NONE BUT LUCIFER

THE INQUIRY into uncharted domains of the outer and inner human cosmos has been a central issue of the very best in science fiction and fantasy literature for over fifty years—long before the mainstream SF drifted into technophile cloak & dagger adventures. Besides being of eminent metaphysical interest, many of the science fiction classics of the golden and silver age are veritable gems of prose fiction.

Gateways Retro SF is dedicated to the preservation of the very best writings of the pioneers of this genre of American literature.

NONE BUT LUCIFER

by

Horace L. Gold

GATEWAYS RETRO SCIENCE FICTION

© 2002, Gateways Books and Tapes

Some material in this book has appeared in its present form
or earlier textual versions in
Street & Smith's *Unknown*, September 1939

NONE BUT LUCIFER, © 1939 H. L. Gold and L. Sprague de Camp,
© 2002 E.J. Gold

All rights reserved. Printed in the United States of America.
Gateways Books and Tapes
P.O. Box 370
Nevada City, CA 95959
1-800-869 0658
http://www.gatewaysbooksandtapes.com

Cover art by E. J. Gold
Cover design and type layout by iTRANSmedia

With 14 Illustrations by Kirby Carter

Library of Congress Cataloging-in-Publication Data

Gold, H. L. (Horace Leonard), 1914-
None but Lucifer / by Horace L. Gold.
    p. cm. -- (Gateways retro science fiction)
ISBN 0-89556-128-X (alk. paper)
I. Title. II. Series.
PR9199.3.G5975 N66 2002
813'.54--dc21

                                                2002005651

ISBN 0-89556-128-X

Contents

He glared at the door, as if that would make it open sooner.

Chapter I

HALE HAD PLENTY of reason for panic. Most men, lying sick, broke, and alone in a cheap, filthy rooming house, would have been terrified. But Hale wasn't. He was sick, broke, and alone, all right—only that was exactly how he wanted to be. A long time ago he had planned it. Having achieved what superficially appears to be an easy goal, he felt rather successful. He waited impatiently for the next step in his campaign.

He listened to the stairs. He had been listening since early morning. His hungry, wan face brightened. They were creaking, in the exact manner he had anticipated.

The two pairs of feet plodded irresolutely toward his door. Then they halted. Hale listened impatiently for the creaking to resume. Instead he heard muffled, excited whispering.

He fought down his exasperation. If he had dared to expose his eagerness, he would have cried: "I know it's you and your wife, Burke, coming to dispossess me, if you can get me out while you put a slug in my lock. Don't worry about that. Don't waste time thinking up clever schemes to lure me out. I've waited for years for the courage to put myself in this position. You're not going to fail me because of a little pity, are you? Please, man...my destiny's getting restless."

Naturally, he kept silent. He knew the vigilance of his oppressor too well; he had spent years coaching himself against such revealing outbursts. But in spite of himself he dragged his head off the hot pillow. "Come on!" he wished feverishly. "Don't make me wait!"

He glared at the door, as if that would make it open sooner. What was keeping them?—he ranted to himself. Was it their business that he had to be dispossessed? They were only janitors. They'd had to do it before.

They wouldn't have to trick him out. He'd just get up, dress, and leave. Perhaps he should make some feeble protest, for the sake of appearance. That was all. And he'd be on the street, penniless with no idea of what to do next—just as he'd planned so minutely—just as he wanted so wholeheartedly that he could hardly keep still.

The stairs creaked again. "Come on, come on," he willed furiously. "Don't stop. Please don't stop—"

Mrs. Burke was fumbling through her apron pockets for the keys. Hale could hear the rustle of enamel-stiff starch, the strangled clink of the keys, and Mr. Burke's hoarse, adenoidal mouth-breathing.

The grim janitress searched the ring for the exact key. Hale suspected that a toothpick would have worked as well. The owner of the house spent damned little time worrying about his tenants' possessions, and less money on locks.

Eager as he was to be put out, Hale was flattered by the janitors' reluctance. It couldn't be habitual with them, or they wouldn't have been superintendents for twenty-five years. It meant that they liked and pitied him. He could have enjoyed the sensation of being liked, except that it was hindering instead of helping him just now.

"Stop fumbling!" he hissed under his breath.

The lock clicked boldly, as if it actually served to hold the door closed, and then the door was swinging back on its own flimsy weight. Like two pall-bearers who had embarrassingly arrived before the patient was dead, the Burkes edged into the dark little room.

"How...gh—" Mrs. Burke gulped. "How are you, sir?"

"I'm fine, but what's the matter with you?" Hale's thin voice rose to feeble irascibility. "You could have been here hours ago."

Burke closed his perpetually dry mouth for a much-needed swallow. "It's hanged I'll be if I can make you out, Mr. Hale. You're sick as a dog. By rights you ought to be in a hospital—"

"Edgar!" his wife broke in.

"I know it ain't a nice thing to say. All the same, I want you to let me call an ambulance. It won't cost you anything, Mr. Hale. You'll go in the charity ward."

Mrs. Burke nodded. "We can't throw you out on the

street right at the beginning of February. You come from a good family and you ain't used to the cold. Besides, you're real sick."

"Just a little flu," said Hale. "Please help me get my feet out of bed. They're rather heavy."

"Why don't you be reasonable, Mr. Hale?" Burke pleaded. "Molly here don't mind taking care of you, but, hell, she can't do it like a hospital can. In no time you'll be—"

"Will you help me get my feet out, or shall I do it myself?"

"Oh, nuts!" Burke grunted helplessly. "I got an idea you really want to be thrown out." He lifted Hale's legs around.

Hale froze in a sitting position. Was he being obvious? If Burke could suspect his impatience, his enemy certainly could.

"You're wrong," he said with deliberate primness. "I was brought up to believe in paying my way. I can't pay my rent, so I don't deserve to stay. And I won't take charity."

He was relieved to see that his logic stopped them temporarily. As firmly as he could, he stood up. The blood swooped down from his head and his knees sagged. He caught Burke's shoulder.

"Aw, don't be a fool," Burke implored.

Hale managed to shake his head. The temptation was enormous. He knew he needed a soft, clean bed, decent food, and medical attention. He wanted them so much.

He pushed himself erect. "I'm all right now." He took off his pajama jacket and let it slide to the floor. Mrs. Burke stood by uncertainly. When Hale reached for the pants tape, she went outside.

"Where are you going when you get out of here?" Burke pursued doggedly.

Hale shrugged. "I have plans."

Gently, Burke helped him pull his underwear jersey over his head. "Yeah? What kind?"

"Business plans. I don't think it would be good luck to talk about them."

"I think you're nuts. It's delirious you are."

Bending over his shoes, Hale stopped short. That was a possibility, he had to admit.

Then he grinned up at Burke and went on tying his laces. Ridiculous! He went back over his recent past. Methodically, he had outlined a course of action.

Following it scrupulously, he had given up a forty-a-week job—a very secure one, with the chance of rising to sixty and retiring eventually on half pay. His fiancée had been outraged, naturally. Even so, she trusted his judgment and had hung on.

Did he love her? Well, he had once. At least, she had appealed to him. She was pretty. And she was nice. Maybe that was the trouble. Too nice. Girls like that came in droves. For a nice fellow, a nice girl, a nice job, a nice future, a nice home, nice children.

But Hale couldn't be content with these nice things. He couldn't cut the coat of his ambition to fit his abilities.

So he had conceived his bizarre plan. He had carefully taken his savings and bought the most worthless stocks he could find.

For a while he had feared being duped into making a profit. But his plan had worked, and he had succeeded in selling out just before the stocks in question went up. The memory of that nervous time still made him sweat. But playing the market had accomplished two major objectives: his embarrassing savings were gone, and Loretta with them. It had been worth the anxiety.

"All right?" Mrs. Burke called through the door.

"Yep. Come on in," Hale answered cheerfully.

She watched him writhe into his overcoat with obvious disapproval. Before he put his hat on, she looked encouragingly at her husband.

"See here, Mr. Hale," Burke suddenly blurted, "we ain't exactly millionaires, but we got hearts." He held out a five-dollar bill.

It was a tough moment for Hale. Instead of virtuously protesting, however, he drew several coins out of his own pocket, removed the single penny, and held out three quarters to Mrs. Burke.

"I know it doesn't repay you for the way you've taken care of me," he said clumsily, "but when I'm in a better position I'll really make it up to you. Please take it."

Mrs. Burke began to cry into her apron. "He's crazy!" she wailed. "Seventy-six cents is all he's got in the world. I know, because that's the change I brought him when I got his medicine. And he wants to keep a penny and give me seventy-five cents!"

Burke, looking shocked, moved determinedly toward Hale. "Take this! You're not leaving the house without it!"

"Please don't excite me," Hale gasped, retreating. "I can't take it. It would make me unhappy."

His agitation persuaded Mrs. Burke to call off her husband. His goggling horror of being forced to take the money was real enough to have convinced anyone.

Burke regretfully put the bill away. They stood around awkwardly. Hale, for all his peculiarities, lacked the consummate heartlessness to dash away abruptly, much as he wanted to be off.

"What about your luggage?" Mrs. Burke asked huskily.

"Why...you're going to keep them, of course. I haven't paid my rent—"

Burke snapped his mouth closed. For several seconds he looked quite fierce, glowering with wounded pride at Hale. In the end, naturally, he was forced to open his mouth again to breathe. "None of that, now," he threatened.

"But it's your right to hold them," Hale protested.

"I don't care if it is. I won't."

Hale thought quickly. Perhaps the idea of getting sick hadn't been so good. It raised too many unforeseen problems, like this one. He had counted on having the superintendent of whatever rooming house he landed in confiscate his belongings.

"Well," he said hopefully, "how about keeping them until I can redeem them?"

"Not a chance!"

"Then until I call for them," Hale amended despairingly. "I'm not strong enough to carry them around."

Suspecting a trap, the Burkes hesitated, but at last agreed. "But no nonsense now!" said Mrs. Burke. "When you need anything, you come right here and get it."

"Certainly. You bet. It's awfully nice of you—" He moved toward the door.

Burke said, "You can't go looking for a job like that." He took Hale's feeble arm and guided him to the tiny square of mirror hanging over the unsteady chest of drawers. "It's like hell you look—see?"

Hale had to smile triumphantly. His face was even better than he had hoped: thin, haggard cheeks; feverishly bright dark eyes; the skin of his high forehead stretched tautly over his skull; his large broken nose jutting out of a tangle of black whiskers; his dry, thin hair standing up. He nodded at the reflection. Excellent, he thought.

"You can use my razor," Burke offered.

Hale winced involuntarily. His stubble of beard was something to be observed at all costs. "No, thanks," he choked out.

He couldn't risk more offers of help by waiting around. Mrs. Burke's mouth was trembling with some suggestion. Before it could come out, Hale squeezed Burke's shoulder, kissed Mrs. Burke's large cheek, and fled.

On the street, he could feel really successful. The bitter wind slashed at him; he had only seventy-six cents and no place to sleep. He was getting somewhere!

Chapter II

HALE DIDN'T STAND indecisively on the cold street. It was not yet noon, and before nightfall he had a fairly rigid course of action to follow.

His brown sport shoes felt like ton weights, he had been out of them for so long; and his overcoat dragged his shoulders down. He knew his temperature was over a hundred, but it did not affect his sharp reasoning.

He felt the sheathed hunter's knife and the pistol in his overcoat pockets, and he smiled with amused anticipation.

They were important. At the start of his campaign he had

selected them with care. But they would not be useful for several days, and then only to prove a point that might be debated.

He walked over to Sixth Avenue and turned downtown. At Fifty-Ninth Street he met the first cluster of men. He squeezed in among them.

"I don't feel despondent enough," he thought analytically. "I don't have the look of defeat."

Not all the men in front of the employment agency were shabby. Some had been thrust down only recently. They glanced almost furtively at the job notices, as if they were merely curious. But there were others, whom Hale studied like an actor learning a role.

They were the habitual prowlers of the agencies, ragged, filthy, too close to starvation to be hungry, shuffling mechanically from hopelessness to indifference. Hale coveted that attitude. He thoughtfully set out to make himself despondent.

How long would his seventy-six cents keep him? A dime for breakfast, fifteen cents for lunch, a quarter for supper— fifty cents for one day. A quarter for a cheap hotel cot.

He could live for one day and have a penny left over. Then what? He had to eat and sleep, and one night on the subway would turn his deep-seated cold into pneumonia. A surge of desperation, which he stealthily enjoyed, gripped him.

He elbowed through the circle of men, and his eyes jumped from one job to another.

Nothing. Industrial jobs: third engineers, Diesel men, oilers, little-way stitchers, plant and factory jobs. He shuffled wearily to the next agency. Restaurant help: countermen, $18. Too high. Dishwashers, colored, $10. Soda dispensers, exp., $18-22.50.

He climbed the narrow, dark stairs to the huge bare room with its hard, shaky benches around three walls and its stench of wet rot and stale smoke. Nothing could fight down that combination. He felt the remnant of his cheeriness strangle.

Timidly, he approached the girl behind the railing.

"What job?" she asked casually.

"The dishwasher."

She glanced at the list. "Colored?"

"N-no. But I can wash just as well as—"

"Sorry. They want colored washers." And she turned away.

"I can make sodas," he blurted hoarsely. "I'm not so good, but—"

"Sorry," she said, her voice remote. "All filled."

He buttoned his coat, left, and trudged down to the next agency.

White chalk on a black slate. Each one, unseen, a block away, was the job, the means of feeding and sheltering himself. But it never was.

There was the application that he made out for a night porter, $12. The girl read it.

"Six dollars in advance, please," she said, quite businesslike.

Hale stopped breathing. "Six dollars! What for?"

"Half our fee. You pay the other half when you get your salary."

"But," he protested, "I haven't *got* six dollars—"

Without glancing at him, she tossed his application into the basket and turned to the next client. He clung to the railing, stunned. The other unemployed looked disinterestedly at him. Didn't they understand, damn them, that he could work and pay his way, six dollars or no six dollars? Why didn't they smash—

13

But, of course, he said nothing. No one ever does. You stand for a moment while they ignore you; then you trudge slowly out without feeling, unconscious of the stairs under your feet and the employment-agency smell—as Hale did.

In the afternoon, Hale did wangle a try-out at an eight-dollar-a-week job as an upholsterer's apprentice from an agency without the advance payment.

The upholsterer was far from enthusiastic when he learned Hale's age—thirty-one—and his lack of experience at manual work.

He watched with suppressed exasperation Hale's bungling efforts to adapt his stiff muscles to the unaccustomed craft. When Hale tried to borrow five dollars, he turned him down cold.

Hale quit. There was nothing else he could do. The agency would get his first week's salary. To keep alive for the first two weeks would require at least twelve dollars, and he had seventy-one cents.

The upholsterer shrugged. "Maybe it's best this way. You wouldn't learn so fast. Not your fault—just too old."

Hale decided that he had gone about far enough. He'd finish off with a night in a Bowery flophouse. He could have had a quarter bed around Sixth Avenue, but the flophouse sounded more dramatic.

He chose a hammock instead of a cot. Squalor was an essential part of his plan, but vermin weren't. He stripped the case off the pillow, which made it only slightly cleaner, and threw the blankets on the floor under the hammock.

They were slick and faintly stiff with grease, and had a gamy smell. If Washington had used those blankets, they hadn't been aired out since.

14

CHAPTER II

That allowed him to sleep in his clothes, shoes and all. He was dissatisfied with the way his tweeds had retained the remnant of a crease.

He woke late, exhausted and stiff. Most of the men had already left. Hale wondered whether he should immediately go on with his plan.

He decided against it, mainly because he still had forty-six cents. Spending it all on meals that day would be too obvious. He must seem to be trying to make it last.

He soaked his head under the single cold-water faucet. He forebore using the large block of cheap soap; it would have been like lathering himself with a cornerstone. And when he put out his hand for one of the five loathsome towels that had been provided for at least sixty men, he drew back, preferring to let himself dry by evaporation.

He washed three glasses and a porcelain bowl, filled them with water, and sprawled out on a bare cot all day, sopping up as much water as he could.

At noon the clerk demanded another dime. At nightfall, still another. When it grew black, the men shuffled in. By that time Hale was asleep with the deep unconsciousness of a faint.

*Hale stared down at the little man. "I want," he explained,
"to marry your daughter—and a one-hundred-thousand-dol-
lar-a-year job."*

Chapter III

QUITE SMUGLY, he inspected himself in the slop-joint mirror. His ugly stubble had grown long enough to become nicely tangled. His drawn face had lost its feverish flush, and was now clammy and defeated-looking. But the condition of his suit and overcoat gave him the most satisfaction. Anybody could see that he had slept in them.

He ate a twenty-cent breakfast, which, he thought, made him feel needlessly fit. Instead of taking the subway a block away, he walked at a swift pace that he knew he could not maintain, to three stations uptown.

He was pleased when his undue strength left him, and he had to grab the rail, going down the subway stairs, to keep from stumbling.

At Fiftieth Street he got off. The penny in his pocket caused him some anxiety. It would be melodramatic to spend it on gum, he thought. Being down to one penny looked better than making himself completely broke. He kept it.

As he walked over to Madison Avenue, the hopelessly depressed manner that he had been so diligently cultivating slid off like a stripteaser's gown. He entered a magnificent office building.

Nobody stopped him when he resolutely stepped into an elevator. People in places like that were more refined; they merely edged away, taking very small breaths from the opposite direction. He stared around with unabashed interest and gave his floor number in a loud, determined voice.

In the corridor, he stopped at the door marked:

BANNER ADVERTISING CO., INC.
Eugene F. Banner, Pres.

There was nothing timid in his manner. He held the doorknob for a few seconds, thinking, as any salesman would do. Then he went in.

He entered a large and efficient-looking reception room. It was laid out rather like the Sixth Avenue employment agencies, excepting the lack of dirt, smoke, and stench.

The girl at the switchboard looked up with polite interest. It amused Hale—the way her expression froze without actually changing.

"Yes?" she asked distantly.

"I want to see Mr. Banner," he replied firmly.

"Have you an appointment?"

Hale had reached the railing. He opened the gate and walked toward the president's office. "I don't need one."

The girl lost her calm. She jumped up and shrieked, horrified: "You can't go in there!"

"If I can't," Hale said without halting, "Mr. Banner will tell me." And he opened Banner's door and walked in. Nobody stopped him. Nobody knew how. Such things simply don't happen, wherefore there is no traditional course of action in such cases.

The president's office was something to command respect. It was large and light and quiet and tasteful, but above all it was dignified, like Mr. Banner. His gray hair was only a fringe around his massive head, and his rather soft body was no longer lean. But his pince-nez were set precisely on a sharp, straight nose that grew from pink, clean cheeks, and he sat very straight in his chair, reading copy.

He must have heard the door, for he stirred. A moment later he evened the edges of pages with ponderous care and raised his head politely.

Mr. Banner's nerves were delicate instruments. When he saw Hale standing determinedly before his desk, he jumped up, sending his chair over with a frightful crash.

Objectively, Hale watched the president's antics. Banner had cleverly placed himself in such a position that he could, almost without possibility of hindrance, reach the telephone, push his secretary's buzzer, or race around the desk toward the door.

"What do you want?" he demanded.

Hale maintained his dominating position. "I want a job here," he said bluntly, "until I can marry your daughter Gloria."

Until he realized that he was exposing his surprise, Mr. Banner goggled at him. Then he pulled himself together.

"Gloria takes care of her own affairs," he said restrainedly. "I try not to interfere."

It didn't fool Hale. He knew he was being humored. "That isn't the important thing," he said. "I don't know Gloria. I've only seen her picture in the papers. But just the same, I think I'll marry her. She's not bad-looking—quite pretty, in fact. I'll work here until I get to know her better."

Mr. Banner stared fixedly at Hale's face and clothes. He knew that most shabby people become self-conscious and malleable when attention is called to their appearance.

"Naturally," Hale went on undaunted, "I don't want to make a permanent thing of it. Work at its best grows boring. But with Gloria's private means I imagine we can struggle along. You won't live much more than ten or twenty years. Then I'll take over your income. That should be about half a million a year. It'll do."

Banner wagged his head slowly, as with pure wonderment. "I can't do anything about Gloria," he said finally. "What she does is her own affair."

Hale was reasonable. "I'll take care of that. I suppose the job is all you can handle. Well, let's start on that as a—"

"Look here!" said Banner brusquely, coming around the desk. "You don't convince me for a second. I'm not an imbecile, you know."

Hale controlled his expression and stood his ground.

"Give you credit for originality," Banner snapped. "An advertising man respects that. Only, you're not convincing.

Next time, hide the intelligence behind a better mask than a couple of days' beard, and don't talk literately. Understand?"

Hale didn't understand, but he didn't say so. Banner went on: "I need a slogan for White Elephant Blended Rye." He snatched a layout from the desk and held it up before Hale. "I've got a blurb, but I need a slogan. Give me one—quick, now!"

Hale, for the first time, backed up a step. But then he recognized his enemy's hand, and stopped. His bluff was being called. He said desperately: "You'll drink White Elephant Blended Rye and like it."

Banner ran a finger over the layout. "You'll drink White Elephant Blended Rye," he traced over the cut, and beneath it: "and like it. Not strong enough; won't pull. And *like* it! That's better. Pretty good."

Banner motioned Hale to one of the big leather chairs and sat himself down in the other. "I was just about resigning myself to this bunch of junk when you came in. I've got a bunch of cluck writers who are dried out, stale, can't get a fresh idea."

Hale stared at the papers. He made it a point to say the first thing that popped into his mind; short, jerky orders to the consumers.

Banner shuffled the pages together again, this time not with ponderous care. He bounced the edges on the desk, straightening them the way a big poker winner evens a pack of cards. He got up and buzzed for his secretary.

"Hale," he said with humorous disapproval, "I knew you were a phony the minute after you walked into my office. Bums don't stand up for their rights when they look as lousy as you do. They shuffle and whine. That was your mistake.

But I'll say this: You're damned clever. You challenged me to see through your disguise, and I like challenges. There probably isn't a better judge of men than I am. Tell you how I knew you weren't a real bum: The soles of your shoes weren't worn through!"

Hale grinned unashamedly, and his grin flattered Banner, who, of course, hadn't had a chance to see the soles of Hale's shoes until he had told Hale to sit down.

Banner went on: "I really can't do anything about my daughter. But I *will* give you a job. Fifty a week. That's just a starter."

Still grinning, Hale shook his head. "I want a hundred thousand a year."

Banner choked, but came up laughing between coughs. "I must say, when it comes to plain, unvarnished gall, you've got me beaten. Thought I was pretty good. I'll make it five thousand a year. That's final."

"A hundred thousand."

Hale's set grin began to irk Banner. "You're serious, aren't you? Well, get it out of your mind. I can stand crust, but you're talking like a lunatic. Ten thousand."

Hale opened his mouth. What he intended to say was not very clear, but at that instant a man entered.

"Mason," said Banner curtly, "this is Hale."

"How do you do, Mr. Hale," replied Mason uncertainly. He made a couple of imperceptible motions with his right hand, as if unable to decide whether to offer it.

"I've just hired Hale," Banner continued. "Give him a fifty-dollar advance on his salary. Take him around to my barber and my tailor, and give him the works. Get him a steam bath and a rubdown at my club. And you, Hale, take the day off. Get yourself an apartment you won't be ashamed of, and be at work at ten tomorrow. No, come back here before closing, say at four. That's all."

Hale put his battered hat on jauntily. "You're a shrewd, hard man, Mr. Banner. I'll get the better of you yet."

"Just try it," replied Banner confidently. "You'll be the first."

Without seeming too obviously distant, but contriving to look as if they were accidentally going the same way, Mason steered Hale out of the office.

Hale stepped into a pawnshop to come out ten minutes later in an ill-fitting hand-me-down.

Chapter IV

ALONE AGAIN, Hale ambled along Park Avenue. He carefully avoided enjoying his cleanliness and his clothes. To him they were scientific instruments, like the gun and the knife, which he had transferred to the pockets of his new overcoat.

He was another step further in his campaign, but he didn't mistake the means for the end. His ten-thousand-a-year job and his clothes were neither more nor less important than the whiskers he had raised and the night he had spent in the flophouse. They were all necessary parts of the plan.

He stopped at a high, creamy, clean-looking apartment house and sought out the renting agent, a breathlessly enthusiastic young woman.

"Something not too ostentatious," she judged, studying his appearance. "Not too large."

"No," he contradicted gently. "Quite large. An entire floor. I'd prefer a penthouse."

"I have *just* the thing! The top floor is vacant. Isn't that *lucky*? Oh, you'll *love* it! It's simply *ador*able!"

By normal standards it was several sizes too large to be adorable. Counting servants' quarters, solarium, and gymnasium, it was twenty-nine rooms.

"Not bad," he said languidly. "I believe it will do."

"Oh, how splendid!" the agent gushed. "I *knew* you'd love it. Have you seen the view?" She herded him out to the promenade on top of the first setback. "It isn't very clear today, but when it is, you can see *ever* so far over New Jersey, Long Island—and the Bronx," she finished lamely. "I'm sure you'll be de*lir*iously happy here. How soon would you like to take occupancy?"

"Immediately. I'll have the furniture sent up. You'll supervise its placing, of course."

"Of *course!* I just *love* to arrange furniture."

"When the car comes, let it stand outside the door. Show the chauffeur his room. The servants will arrive shortly. One of them will ask you for a floor plan. Give it to him. I believe that's all."

She trailed hesitantly after him. "Mr. Hale, I don't know how to put it—"

He stared coldly at her. When she merely looked embarrassed, he said: "Of course, the money. My secretary will take care of it through my office. Call Banner Advertising Co. for references."

"Oh, I hope you don't mind. It's just a formality, you know. You *do* understand, don't you, Mr. Hale?"

The maroon car was enormously long and sleek—the one car that would stand out on Park Avenue. Hale entered the agency and told the salesman that that was the car he wanted.

"You'll be completely satisfied with it, sir," the man promised. "We can give you almost immediate delivery. Three weeks."

"I'm not in the habit of waiting," Hale replied frigidly. "This is the car I want. I'll take it now."

The salesman swallowed uneasily. "That isn't customary, sir."

"I don't care if it isn't. I'll take this car as soon as you can get it out of the window."

"I'll have to speak to the manager—"

"And tell him," Hale said frostily, "that this will be a cash transaction."

While the salesman whispered awedly to the manager, Hale gazed indifferently at the car. The manager came over and said: "We'll be delighted to let you have our display car, sir. Of course, it will take an hour or so to remove. Suppose we have it delivered to you. Will that be all right, sir?"

"Fine," said Hale unenthusiastically.

"You spoke of a cash transaction, sir—"

"Naturally. My secretary will arrange the details. You may call Banner Advertising Co."

"Banner, sir? I'm sure everything is all right. But, you

understand, I really must call them. Just routine, you know."
A moment later he was talking very respectfully into the
instrument, his pleased face nodding. Then he beamed.
"Everything is settled, Mr. Hale. Mr. Banner would like to
speak to you."

Hale took up the telephone. "Hello."

"What the hell are you doing, Hale?" Banner cried. "First
I get a call from a Park Avenue apartment house asking if
you're responsible, and now I get a call from this car company. Just what—you're not getting a hundred thousand, you
know. I know you've got big ideas, but aren't you going way
over your means?"

"I know," Hale said smoothly. "I can handle it. Don't
worry about me, Mr. Banner."

"Well, if you think you're doing right," said Banner
doubtfully. "Oh, hell! Of course you know what you're
doing. Just don't overplay your hand. Go ahead."

Hale hung up, arranged for a chauffeur with the manager,
and left. The manager and salesman saw him out, leering
politely.

Hale reasoned that, while his clothes and his job helped,
the real secret lay in the manner. For example, the more servants he demanded, the less the woman who ran the domestic
employment agency would question his financial standing.

You look at her without the slightest touch of warmth or
intimacy, and you say, as Hale did: "I want a complete staff for
a twenty-nine-room apartment. The chauffeur is already hired.
The others I will leave to you."

And she cries gratefully: "Oh, yes, sir. We take only servants with the very best references."

"Splendid," you reply unemotionally. "The ones I demand

perfection in are the chef—I do a great deal of entertaining—
and the butler and the valet. They must be the most efficient
ones you have."

She darted to the waiting room with the alertness of a spar-
row, and produced two men in snug black coats, with appro-
priately distant expressions and authentic London accents.
These she introduced as Cummings, butler, and Hamilton,
valet. "I'm sure you'll be completely satisfied, Mr. Hale."

"Yes, I'm sure I shall," Hale replied disinterestedly.

He wrote an address on a card and gave it to Cummings.
"Ask the renting agent there for the floor plan. Go to some
first-rate furniture place and buy what is needed for each
room. Insist on floor samples. I can't wait for them to make
the furniture. However, if I do not like what you buy, I shall
return it and order something more suitable. I want everything
delivered by five o'clock. That should be ample time. You
have slightly less than three hours."

"Yes, sir," said Cummings. His frozen face was as nearly
pleased as it ever could be. Hale had discovered that giving
others responsibility for arranging everything was the surest
way of taking their minds off money. "How shall I arrange
payment, sir?"

"My secretary will take care of it. You, Hamilton, settle
matters with the gas and electric company." He drew out the
remainder of the fifty dollars, counted it, and asked the owner
of the agency to change a dollar bill. He still had the original
penny. To that he added three quarters, and gave the rest to
Hamilton. "That's all I can spare at the moment. Make that do
as a deposit."

Hamilton gravely accepted the money. "Will that be all,
sir?"

"Certainly not. Bring the staff to the address I gave

29

Cummings. Order food. Have the chef prepare dinner for seven thirty; whatever his specialty is. By that time I want all the furniture in order."

He passed time strolling; it was a few minutes after four when he returned to the apartment house. He glanced at the car standing at the curb, and called the chauffeur downstairs. Getting in, he said: "North shore of Long Island. Schedule the ride so we shall return by seven."

Hale lolled on the broad seat, deliberately unconscious of the car's smoothness and luxurious upholstery. They purred over the Queensboro Bridge. The day lost its chill brightness; darkness seeped through the air. Driving in complete silence, the chauffeur had glanced several times at the clock on the instrument board. Then, without a word, he turned the car and headed back to New York.

At seven, having neither enjoyed nor disliked the ride, Hale strode through his new home. The butler followed him at a respectful distance, proud, in a dignified, inarticulate way, of his speed and taste.

"Quite nice," Hale said, as one would applaud a clever dog. "I doubt if I shall have to exchange a thing."

"I am glad you like it, sir," said Cummings, frozenly delighted.

Hamilton appeared. "Would you care to dress for dinner, sir? I couldn't find your wardrobe."

"Not tonight, Hamilton. Everything is too unsettled."

"Then, sir," Cummings said, "the chef has informed me that dinner is ready. He has made terrapin. His terrapin, sir, is famous. Mr. Astor admitted it."

Hale sat down at the enormous table. "Ah, terrapin. Fine. But I want no cocktails or hors d'oeuvres. Just a very large glass of tomato juice."

He drank it. For once Cummings was almost startled when, a few minutes later, Hale stood up.

"Aren't you going to finish your dinner, sir?" he asked, dismayed.

"I don't believe I will. I feel the need of a stroll. For some reason my appetite has left me."

"The excitement of moving, no doubt, sir," Cummings said with reserved sympathy. "Will you want the car?"

"No. Just my coat and hat. Perhaps my appetite will return."

"Oh, yes, sir, I'm sure it will."

Very competent, Hale thought tranquilly. Everything ran smoothly at his slightest desire. Hamilton was helping him on with his coat. The elevator had already been called.

He went down and walked east to Lexington, where he took the subway. If he had allowed himself any emotion, he would probably have regretted his decision not to spend the night in a soft bed. But he did not. His one anxiety was to find a pawnshop open at that hour on the Bowery, where he got out.

They were all open. He entered one, and said: "I want to exchange all my clothes."

The owner stared suspiciously at him. "Take off your coat," he ordered nastily. Then he walked all around, inspecting the suit. "No bloodstains?"

"Bloodstains?" Hale asked. "Of course not."

"Well, it's up to you, mister. If you wanna swap a swell outfit like 'at, I'm not kicking, see? Go ahead and pick out the one you want."

Hale quickly chose a suit, hat, and overcoat. When he came out, even the predatory pawnshop owner felt uneasy. He said: "You can get a better fit than that off the rack."

"No, this'll do," replied Hale decisively. "But, of course, I want the difference in value."

"Oh," said the pawnbroker, putting his hands behind his back. "How much?"

"A dollar and a quarter."

"*Huh?*" The pawnbroker recovered from his surprise and snatched a dollar and a quarter out of the cash drawer, shoved it under the cage, and incredulously watched Hale pocket it. "Come again, mister," he invited as Hale turned away.

"Not much chance. But where can I put an ad in the paper? Is there a place around here?"

"The candy store at the corner takes ads. You better hurry. It's kinda late for the morning papers."

Hale could feel the broker's relief when he left without changing his mind. He smiled; there was small chance of that. In the candy store he asked for a form and a pencil.

"You're too late on the classifieds for the morning papers," said the old man. "You can make an afternoon paper, though."

"O.K.," said Hale. "The *Globe* will do."

He wrote:

TO NONE BUT LUCIFER: OF ALL THE INHABITANTS OF THE INFERNO, NONE BUT LUCIFER AND I KNOW THAT HELL IS HELL.
WILLIAM HALE.

The old proprietor counted the words, stopped in the middle and glanced at Hale, started at the beginning again and counted them through, and said: "That'll be a dollar and a quarter."

"I know," said Hale. "I figured that out several years ago."

CHAPTER IV

He left, grinning, and headed for the flop house. That was the final step in his plan. Everything he had done had led inevitably up to that advertisement.

"Put it away!" howled Johnson. "It might go off!" Hale grinned. "Not with you at the other end of it. It'll misfire."

Chapter V

THE PLACE AMAZED HALE. Just what he had expected was not very clear. But it would have seemed more fitting if it had been luxurious, enormous, of course, dark with furtive shadows, the air heavy with deadening incense. And there should have been only one person present—a lank, intent, mocking figure in flowing black, whose piercing eyes would probe the mind's foulest impulses, whose mouth would sneer perpetually.

Hale stepped out of the shaky elevator into the loft. It was enormous, as lofts usually are. But it was glaringly bright, deafeningly noisy, and full of hard-working men and girls. The floor was rough and unvarnished. All down the length of the huge room, office workers typed, ran calculators, and roved among hundreds of steel filing cabinets.

For the first time, Hale felt uncertain. He was sure that the wrong person had answered his advertisement. But he had addressed it, as emphatically as possible, to one individual only. Nobody else could have made enough sense out of it to answer it.

He approached the harried switchboard operator. "You answered my ad in the *Globe*."

"Hello," she said into the transmitter. "Alexander P. Johnson. I'm sorry, Mr. Johnson is very busy. I'll connect you with one of his assistants."

"My name is William Hale," he said more loudly.

"Hello, Finchley? Mr. Johnson is still interested in the Osterman case...He knows he committed suicide...He wants the inside on their financial condition and what they're going to do with the daughter...Keep in touch there—"

Hale shoved the clipped advertisement at her, jiggling it until her eyes focused on it. "Mr. Johnson's expecting you," she rattled off finally. "Room down at the other end." She pointed at the beaverboard inclosure at the opposite end of the loft, and resumed her steady talking into the telephone and yanking and inserting plugs.

Hale snatched up his ad and strode between the rows of desks. Nobody looked at him. The place was incredibly efficient. He shook his head, puzzled. More than ever he felt he was in the wrong place. He knocked at a door lettered:

CHAPTER V

ALEXANDER P. JOHNSON

Just that, as if it should be obvious who Alexander P. Johnson was. A hearty, businesslike voice invited him to enter.

Alexander P. Johnson sat at a battered, heaped desk. Very little noise came through the insulated beaverboard walls.

Hale stared suspiciously at the mild blue eyes that Alexander P. Johnson raised. Was *this* his goal? This chubby Babbitt with a face like a pale-pink pumpkin, who ran an oversized clipping bureau?

"How do you do," said Johnson, professionally cordial. "You wanted to see me?" He removed his spectacles with a quick gesture.

Hale said: "I put an ad in the *Globe* a couple of days ago, addressed to none but Lucifer. You answered it."

"Did I?" Johnson thrust the earpieces of his glasses into his white hair and scratched the faintly visible pink scalp. "May I see the reply advertisement?"

Hale put it on the desk. Johnson put on his glasses and read aloud:

William Hale: My detective agency and clipping bureau will be of inestimable aid to you. Consult me at your leisure; no obligation. Alexander P. Johnson.

Johnson thought a moment and said: "I don't seem to remember this. What did your advertisement say?"

"To none but Lucifer: Of all the inhabitants of the Inferno, none but Lucifer and I know that Hell is Hell."

"Oh, now I understand," Johnson smiled brightly. "One of my assistants must have answered it. We often reply to classified advertisements, even the obscure ones. The cost is small, and one lucrative case pays for many wasted follow-ups."

Hale looked thoughtfully at Johnson's perfectly ordinary round face. His feelings and his logic were in conflict; but having let his logic lead him thus far, he saw no reason to change his plan now. "You're not convincing me—*Lucifer!*"

Johnson cocked his head. "What...what do you mean?"

"I'll tell you exactly what I mean. My ad was addressed to nobody else. It didn't ask a question, and didn't require a reply. Nobody but Lucifer could have had the slightest interest in it. Your detective agency couldn't have thought I was searching for anyone, and your clipping bureau had no excuse to think I was saving clippings."

"Answering classified advertisements is part of my office's routine—"

Hale leaned over the desk. *"You are Lucifer!"*

Johnson looked frightened. "You're actually taking this nonsense seriously. Please, Mr. Hale...if I've offended you by answering your ad, please accept my apology—"

Hale dragged over the wooden chair behind him and sat down. "You're clever, Lucifer. But I've studied your works too well to be fooled. I'm ashamed of myself for thinking you'd be tall and sinister, with a black cape, horns hoofs, and so forth. That would be melodramatic—obvious. And you're anything but obvious."

Johnson reached toward a board of buttons. "Mr. Hale," he said frantically, "I'm sorry, but if you persist in acting insane, I'll have to ring for assistance."

Hale grabbed Johnson's fat wrist and squeezed. Johnson cried out and his pudgy white hand turned red. Hale rasped:

"I'm probably taking a chance of going out in a puff of smoke, but you're not going to ring if I can help it."

"I won't ring, only just don't squeeze my hand anymore. Please!"

Hale released him. He was slightly shaken by the contact of the warm, soft flesh. It could have belonged to any aging, unathletic businessman, whereas Hale felt that the wrist really ought to have been cold, clammy, and inhumanly strong.

"I'll start at the beginning," Hale said, settling back. "Several writers gave me the hint, but there was always something odd and constrained about the way they dropped their suggestions.

"Arnold Bennett was the main source. You'd expect me to find the truth in some old sorcerer's manuscript, wouldn't you? But those old boys had lost themselves in a mystic maze of absurdity—incantations, charms, and what not. I don't have to explain that to you. You're in a better position to know than anyone else."

Johnson squirmed uncomfortably. His terrified gaze commuted between Hale's fierce eyes and the bulges in his overcoat pockets.

"Bennett was writing his journal. Suddenly, without any connection at all, he put down: 'Of all the inhabitants of the Inferno, none but Lucifer knows that Hell is Hell.' Just like that—no explanation—a random thought—*on the surface!*

"But something—*you!*—kept him from developing that thought and killed him, I suppose, not long after, to prevent him from thinking about it.

"The quotation doesn't explain anything, by itself, but it implies that the damned don't know they're in Hell. They think they're somewhere else. Where?

"At first I wasn't certain. Bernard Shaw gave me the

proof. He said: 'If the planets are inhabited, the Earth is their Hell.' You didn't kill him, but somehow he forgot to develop the idea.

"Now I had the generalizations, and I needed substantiating facts. I used myself as a guinea pig. I arranged to be sick, alone, and broke in a rooming house; but I wanted to escape and find myself homeless on the streets in the middle of winter.

"The superintendent and his wife almost refused to let me go. They'd have put me in a hospital, where I'd have had free food, shelter, and medical attention, if I'd let them. They'd have given me money or let me stay in their apartment.

"But anybody who's lived in a rooming house knows that janitors are completely hardboiled. They don't mind evicting a sick person—when he's scared and wants to stay. You get the opposite of what you want—or *appear* to want.

"So I went to the employment agencies, and sincerely tried to get a job, no matter what sort of work or how little it paid. There were jobs all right. Most of them paid just about enough to live on, but I wasn't particular. Only they wanted deposits, and I didn't have any money.

"I did wangle an eight-dollar-a-week job out of an agent without a deposit. But I wanted that job too much. I got it under conditions that made it impossible to hold it, and pretty soon I was back on the street again.

"So I slept in a flop house and let myself get to look like hell. Then I went after a hundred-thousand-a-year job. But I went at it obliquely. Looking like a bum, I pretended not to want the job for itself so much as for a chance of marrying the boss's daughter.

"According to all the rules, the boss ought to have had me

thrown out as a nut. But he practically forced the job on me, though I all but refused it. Or should I say *because* I all but refused it? I still don't know just what he expected me to do—something in the advertising business, which I don't know a damn thing about.

"Then, without paying a cent, I rapidly acquired a huge apartment, a staff of servants, and a beautiful car. I didn't want them particularly—at least, that was the way I acted.

"If I'd wanted them desperately, you know what chance I'd have had of getting them. To show how little I cared for them, I finally abandoned them and hocked my new clothes to pay for the ad, though I could just as easily have kept back more than seventy-six cents.

"All of which shows that if you want something badly enough, you may get it. But it won't make you happy. It may take your whole lifetime—in fact, it usually does, just so it'll arrive when you can't enjoy it or when it'll seriously embarrass you."

Johnson was still looking apprehensively at the bulging pockets in which Hale kept his hands. "I'm sure that's very interesting. I don't see—"

"Oh, yes, you do. The Founding Fathers were a lot more practical than the medieval wizards. What does the Declaration of Independence say? '—inalienable right to the *pursuit* of happiness.' They knew better than to give the right to happiness, because they knew that only the *pursuit* is possible.

"But the ancient Greeks were the ones who had really studied life. Instead of a lot of childish brimstone, bats, and eternal coal shoveling, they pictured Hell as a place of psychological torment.

"There's Sisyphus, eternally pushing his boulder up a hill.

Every so often he tires, and the boulder rolls down to the bottom, and he has to start over. There is no summit to the hill, but Sisyphus doesn't know that. Nor has he thought about what it'll be like if he does get to the nonexistent top.

"In real life some rare Sisyphus does sometimes perch his boulder on the peak of some hill. Then he either realizes what a stupid waste of effort it was, or, worse, he sees other, bigger hills with even more magnificent boulders to roll up them. Those, he thinks, will be success at last.

"*Yeah*!

"Then there's Tantalus, starving and dying of thirst, up to his neck in a pool of cool, clean water, with a gorgeous cluster of fruit just in reach. He bends over to drink, and the water recedes.

"He reaches for the fruit, and the bough sways just far enough away to keep it out of reach. Sometimes he actually touches it; that keeps him trying. At last, when he's close enough to death, he succeeds!

"The fruit, of course, is dry, tasteless pulp."

Johnson fidgeted silently with a stack of paper for a minute. "How does that concern me?"

"Well, you can see the analogies. All of us suffer like Sisyphus and Tantalus, either in the realization of the meaninglessness of success, or in not attaining it. In short, the earth we're living on is Hell.

"We don't have to die; *we're already there*. I don't know what we're paying for, nor where we committed the remarkable sins that seem to require such vicious punishment.

"All I know is that if this is Hell, it's a damnably efficient one. From the time we're born until we die, we suffer unbearable tortures—physical, mental, and spiritual; but most of all, fiendishly ingenious psychological tortures.

"For instance, when we're young we have health and strength and sharp senses. But we haven't the knowledge to use them properly. By the time we've learned to make something of them, we're getting old and losing them, and we know that our knowledge comes too late. Too late—and we know there's no going back; that we'll just get older and feebler until we die. Yet we cling to life.

"That's the greatest psychological torture of all; the instinct of self-preservation, the urge to live at all costs, no matter how much we've suffered or how much we'll continue to suffer as long as we live."

Johnson shook his head. "There's always hope," he said piously.

"Right! You saw to that. First a blind young hope. A few failures blunt that quickly enough, don't they? Then that eager hopefulness becomes a cowed, hopeless hope that maybe things will turn out all right after all. If they don't—there's always hope.

"If success comes and turns out futile and tasteless, there's always hope that it'll be better next time. So we keep on trying and inviting more disappointments.

"There was the oil magnate who hoped to live to a hundred—and died just short of it. There was the aluminum magnate who quit business at seventy, dashed off his memoirs quickly before he died—and then sat on his porch every day for twenty years, waiting for the death he hoped for. Pleasant, isn't it? A fit invention of Lucifer."

"I still don't see how that concerns me."

"Don't you? A Hell as efficient as this needs an organizing genius. It could never run so well without a manager."

Johnson returned Hale's thin smile with a troubled

exposure of obviously false teeth. "And you think I'm the—manager, eh?"

"I don't *think* so. I *know* you're Lucifer!"

Johnson relapsed into apprehensive silence.

"You don't deny it, do you?" Hale accused.

Johnson strangled in an agony of indecision. "I would if you weren't insane! Of...of course I deny it!"

"I came prepared for that," said Hale quietly. He stood up slowly and took out the gun. Johnson looked incredulous, jumped up, and tried to disappear behind the desk. The chair was jammed against the wall. There wasn't space.

"Don't! Don't! Please—"

He couldn't get his head down. It was impossible to miss. Hale took careful aim at the white, bobbing head. If the scrupulously cleaned and oiled mechanism hadn't jammed, he'd have blown that head right off.

Hale grinned and threw the gun away. "I was prepared for that, too. Now, just to make sure it wasn't an accident—" He took out the hunting knife.

He wasn't even slightly nervous as he leaned over the desk, behind which Johnson was shrieking. Holding the sheath in his left hand, he tried to draw the blade with his right. At least a dozen vulnerable points were exposed.

—if the knife hadn't stuck in its sheath.

Just to be certain, Hale yanked again, with all his strength. He didn't expect it to come out. It didn't. Still grinning, he tossed the knife on the floor.

"There," he said. "That's my proof. That gun has never jammed before. It couldn't. With the safety catch off, you could practically shoot it by blowing on the trigger. And who ever heard of a knife sticking in a clean sheath a couple of sizes too big?"

Alexander P. Johnson straightened up. The puffs of white flesh crinkled into a genial network. "I admit it," he said in his hearty businessman's voice. "I'm Lucifer. What's your game, young fellow?"

"That's pretty obvious. I want to go into partnership with you."

Hale had attained his end: what he wanted—was his. His , as soon as he wanted it—anything!

Chapter VI

LUCIFER SAT DOWN, laughing. He didn't roar with diabolical amusement; he used a spasmodic chuckle, as if he
were merely laughing at a story at a businessmen's luncheon.
"I must give you credit," he gasped. "You *do* have a remarkable amount of nerve."

"Why?"

"Well, the idea of coming to Lucifer with a proposition
of that sort. You know who I am, yet you dare ask me for a
partnership. It takes blind, insane courage—"

"Oh, no!" Hale grinned rather smugly. "*I* hold the whip hand, Lucifer. When you do that you don't really need courage."

"Really?" Lucifer leaned forward interestedly. "You have the whip hand over *me*?"

"Precisely, Lucifer."

"I wish you wouldn't call me that. It makes me think of the medieval conception of me, which you described so nastily. I'm not like that at all, really. Please call me Mr. Johnson. And please explain what you mean by that remark about the whip hand."

"Very well, Mr. Johnson. I happen to have the key to your defeat. I can get anything I want any time I want it, and you can't stop me. Moreover, anybody can use my system.

"If you turn me down, I'll pass the system along to as many people as I can. In a little while everybody would be using it and getting anything they wanted. Then where would you be?"

Alexander P. Johnson took out a box of cigars, offered one to Hale, who declined, and lit one himself before answering.

"Well," he finally said, "that's a problem. Yes, sir. Where would I be? Frankly, I don't know. It would upset my careful plans, as you say. But what is your system? Unless, of course, you don't care to show your hand."

Hale shook his head good-humoredly. "I don't mind. You can take a look at the cards, but you can't tell how I'll play them. Get what I mean?"

"I think I do." Johnson tapped the ash off the cigar with a pompous flourish. "You keep me guessing whether you're breaking a pair to fill a straight or going after a full house. Is that it?"

CHAPTER VI

"Well, if you like metaphors, that's my system. I go after what I want obliquely, by seeming to aim at something else, but grabbing sideways at what I actually want. You see?"

"Can you give me a concrete example?"

"I don't know if I should," Hale replied doubtfully.

"That's up to you." Johnson spread his elbows on the desk and twinkled at Hale. "After all, how do I know you really have me cornered?"

That *was* the question, Hale thought; or rather, that was how this very undiabolical Lucifer had chosen to trap him.

He'd have to reveal his secret, which might make it worthless as an instrument of blackmail. But would he have to reveal it? That posed the question of whether Lucifer was the insidious mind reader he was supposed to be.

Here were the facts: During the antics that had led up to his calling on Lucifer, he had kept his mind off his ultimate objective as much as possible.

But he couldn't help an occasional gloat as he saw how his plan was working according to schedule.

Still, until he had bluntly told Lucifer his terms, Lucifer had not known his objective. Which meant that Lucifer was not a mind reader, and had to judge men by their words and acts. So Hale felt confident in parrying:

"Well, I lay out a systematic campaign. I can be aiming at money, fame, love, an easy life, or influence—but I wouldn't show which one I really wanted. You'd have to guess. The only way you could stop me would be by keeping me headed away from all of them."

"I see," said Johnson. "Such as apparently wanting to marry Gloria Banner, but actually going after a job. Or it could be vice versa. Quite clever, I must admit. But doesn't it take more planning than most people would be capable of?"

"Not much. The main thing is to keep your mouth shut about what you really want. The next most important thing is to get out of your social class.

"You can depend on your own class or the one just above it to defeat you—like the way I was kept out of a job because I didn't have a deposit, and then given one I couldn't keep.

"But if you break out of your class, the one you're crashing isn't sure of your aims, and can't crush you so effectively.

"If you're trying to get a job as a clerk, your objective is pathetically simple to figure out. You want to eat. But if you go after a hundred-thousand-a-year position, with a crack at the boss's daughter, it gets tougher to analyze your goal.

"You may want social position, or a soft life on the family income, or a big name, or the money itself.

"In the first case, you'll work under conditions that aren't much better than no job at all, except for the Tantalus hope of a raise. So you'll be made suitably unhappy.

"But in the second, maybe you won't be ecstatic, but at least you'll have security and decent surroundings, and you can arrange your routine the way you like."

Johnson put his thumb in his vest. "Do you really think so?"

"Oh, the rich probably suffer, too. In Hell nobody can be entirely happy. But that isn't the point. My system is good enough to force a partnership out of you."

"Well, I'll admit one thing," said Johnson. "The world is much too large for even my extremely efficient organization to follow every single person.

"Like you, I lay out a plan and depend on the social forces operating on the more influential individuals of the various classes to carry it through.

"If a detail goes wrong, I correct the detail, and the plan

goes through pretty much as I want it.

"With you, though—my design was seriously upset. My statistical department found an upturn in employment, a phenomenon we check carefully. First, you were given a ten-thousand-a-year job—the equivalent of perhaps ten annual wages.

"Then, at least twenty people were given employment through you: your servants, a replacement order on the display car you...uh...bought, the apartment, which had been vacant for over a year, and so forth. Mostly through the medium of credit—since you deferred payment—a sizable quantity of money was set in circulation. That had to be investigated.

"My admirable detective bureau discovered that you were the cause. I also learned about your leaving the rooming house, and your difficulties in trying to get a job, and that directly from a transient hotel of the worst sort, with an extremely unprepossessing appearance, you had gotten that position from Banner, and the new clothes, the car, and all the rest, all of which you abandoned in the most unusual circumstances.

"Frankly, I was puzzled. You could have lived under those pleasant conditions indefinitely, yet you chose not to. It disturbed my plans unbearably. The number of people you influenced would amaze you. I admit I was bewildered, for once in centuries."

Hale sat back, feeling very pleased with himself. It is not given to every man to baffle Lucifer.

"Because of that," Johnson continued, "I'm afraid you've made me suspicious. What troubles me is your goal."

Hale smiled confidently. "Just what I said: A partnership."

"Ah!" Johnson cocked his head. "But *is* it? Up to now you've used your system of indirection to keep me guessing. Don't tell me you're reversing and really saying what you're after?"

"Why not?"

"Well, since I know your method and your objective, I might trick you."

"Not a chance! I don't have a thing to be afraid of."

"Why are you so certain?"

"Because I have you by the throat, that's why. You could concentrate on holding me, alone, down; but what would you do about a hundred, or a hundred thousand, people using my system? You couldn't run the rest of the world!"

Johnson rested his cheeks against his fists. Of all the unsatanic poses he could have struck, this was the most absurdly human. The pressure pushed his mouth into a naive little rosebud. "That's true. Yes, I suppose that is true. Still, abandoning your system of indirection—"

Hale wondered uneasily why Lucifer kept harping on his system. Was he implying something? But Hale was too near his objective to worry much. What could Lucifer do? Nothing! "Well?" Hale demanded brusquely. "Yes or no?"

Johnson stirred. "I was thinking. You're quite right in taking the bold course. I am helpless—*against your system*!" He stood up and held out his fat hand. "I give in. Before you change your mind, I insist on making you my partner, to share control of Hell!"

Hale sprang to his feet and seized the hand. They grinned like a couple of salesmen who have just sold each other a million dollars' worth of goods at fifty percent commission.

The simile was apt. In his triumphant confusion, Hale neglected to analyze Lucifer's concluding speech. If he had, he would have discovered that they had both sold each other a bill of goods.

But especially Lucifer.

Chapter VII

HALE'S SENSE OF VICTORY grew overwhelming. There really was something to be excited about: He was master of half the earth! Lucifer and Hale, partners! The power he imagined himself wielding was heady stuff. He had to fight to maintain his balance.

"What can I count on getting out of this partnership?" he asked almost soberly.

Johnson clapped him on the shoulder. "Responsibility,

my boy. Mainly that. Running the world is a mighty big job, you know."

"I mean for myself."

Johnson smiled knowingly. "A practical, self-seeking fellow. That's fine. The last thing I'd want is an ascetic. What do you want? Power, fame, money, notoriety—watch out for that, by the way. You can imagine how unpleasant it was for me during the Middle Ages."

"All of them," said Hale emphatically, "and as much more as I can get my hands on. First of all, I ought to have a pretty good fortune."

Johnson punched Hale's chest with a stubby forefinger. "Quite right, my boy. Before you can become valuable to me, you must get your personal problems settled. Money is a disturbing factor. You should have enough of it to let you think about other affairs."

"How do I go about getting it?"

"Well, that depends." Johnson cocked his head and gazed abstractedly. "Being my partner doesn't imply black magic, you know. When you want money, you don't mumble some nonsense or mix up a horrible-smelling brew, and *ffft!*—there it is."

Hale's eyebrows shot up.

"Oh, come, William! You ought to know better than that. Running Hell on an efficient basis happens to be my business, and I run it the same as any other businessman runs his business, by practical, common-sense methods."

"Then where's my power?" asked Hale in distress.

"It's there, all right, without a lot of childish magic. It's all the more subtle and effective, I might point out, because you work with common everyday methods.

"I'm immortal, of course. Hence I can control the world's

money simply by investing a little and waiting for the interest charges to pile up. Outside of that, I can run the world merely by a magnificent system of obtaining information, an understanding of men's desires, and a knowledge of how to use pivot men. And, of course, the ability to start and stop the flow of money.

"In most cases the last can be done without a penny. I'll show you how after you give me an estimate of how much you desire."

Hale thought, then said tentatively: "Let's say a few million."

"Fine. That will be an excellent beginning. Follow me and I shall demonstrate my practical methods." He strutted to the door. "I suppose black magic would be convenient at times. Unfortunately nature gives me very little leeway in sorcery. But I've always thought it would be undignified and obvious, anyhow."

He marched pompously through the clattering loft to the enormous files, and indicated the wall of cabinets with a proud gesture. "There is one other as comprehensive as this. That one is in Europe, and is, obviously, mine."

Hale looked admiringly. It *was* gigantic, and the thought of having to use it as efficiently as Lucifer did frighten him. "I don't see how I'll get the hang of it," he admitted.

"It's simplicity itself. A child could run it blindfolded. Here"—he moved heavily to a drawer—

"We're after 'Stock Market.' Occasionally you'll find cross references—the system is a simple affair of cross filing—"

"But so many people!"

"What do you mean?"

"Why, keeping track of everybody—"

"Oh, don't be silly. It's enough to keep track of trade and production and social, political, and economic movements, with the key figures in each category, their influence, their motives and objectives, and what effect certain...uh...stimuli will have on their own categories and on society in general."

He motioned away several office workers who hovered around, and pulled the drawer out on its rollers. Flipping through the A's, he orated: "Here's 'Aircraft Stocks,' with a list and analysis of every owner large enough to affect the market."

He pointed at one name. "This man has powerful allies. For several years he had been...unfortunate in his stock manipulations. You understand. He was anxious to recoup his losses, but cautious. Consequently," Johnson twinkled, "rumors began circulating among his omniscient financial circles.

"He investigated—oh, very secretly, of course—and discovered that the government had authorized the sale of airplanes to friendly nations. On a cash-and-carry basis, but it would still amount to plenty.

"He saw the advantage of controlling the market for aircraft stocks, so he borrowed millions of dollars from his allies."

Hale had listened without much comprehension. "I don't see how that'll help me—"

"I don't expect you to, yet. We could use any of a thousand men to get your fortune. This one will serve a number of purposes.

"Let me continue: By giving this secret information to several influential persons, I can create a tremendous uproar in the newspapers and in Congress. Do you grasp the significance?

"I have sedulously nurtured the policy of isolation. The furor against its violation will intrench it more strongly.

"Within a few minutes after I have revealed the secret, *this* manipulator will be informed. His stocks will toboggan, and he will have to sell as quickly as possible to get from under."

"I see," said Hale, in the tone of one who doesn't see at all. "But what do I do?"

"You? I thought it was obvious." Johnson shoved the drawer back and guided Hale back to his office. He motioned at the telephone. "Ask the operator to get you Titus, Farnsworth & Quinn."

"Thank you," said the operator, and Hale could have sworn that she added: "Mr. Hale." He jerked his head up and stared quizzically at Johnson, who said, "What's the matter?"

"I thought— It's nothing. What do I say?"

Johnson smiled expansively. "Tell them to buy all the aircraft stocks they can get their hands on, after the market has slumped enough to be near bottom. They'll be able to judge. I trained them myself."

"But the market'll be going down—"

"Do as I say. And just tell the girl this is the office of Alexander P. Johnson."

Hale did so. Presently a male voice rumbled: "Hello. Farnsworth speaking."

"Go on," Johnson prompted.

Hale nervously repeated Johnson's instructions.

"Yep. I got that. Any idea how heavy you want to buy?"

Hale put his hand over the transmitter and repeated the question. Johnson said carelessly: "Everything in sight, until the price stops falling."

"Everything in sight until the price stops falling," Hale repeated dutifully.

"Sounds good," said Farnsworth. "I'm sure Mr. Johnson won't mind if we get in on this ourselves a little. Thanks."

Hale hung up cautiously, as if he thought the telephone stand would bite him. He shook his head. "I don't know. Maybe I'm dumb."

"Not at all, my boy. You simply don't have all the facts. This outcry about the violation of our isolation policy will last for several days.

"The small speculators always sell on a falling market and buy on a rising one. The speculator we have set out to strip is cleverer than that; but this time he has over-reached himself by too much borrowing.

"At the end of that time the government will devise an explanation that will soothe everybody, about how by selling aircraft abroad we can step up production, thereby reducing cost per unit and giving our aircraft laboratories facilities for experimentation.

"The furor will subside, and your aircraft stocks will rise even higher than they are now. Incidentally, most of the speculators, having sold short at the bottom of the market to make up their losses somewhat, can be blackmailed splendidly."

"Oh," said Hale.

"There's your first lesson in my methods. No black magic—just detailed information and a knowledge of human nature." Johnson got a check book out of a drawer. "Where do you plan living—at the Park Avenue place?"

Hale drew his hand across his forehead. "I guess so. Once I get used to an apartment a mile square, it'll suit me fine, I suppose. Right now I'm rather dazed."

"Well, you must accustom yourself to big-business methods." Johnson wrote a check and handed it to Hale, who looked at it with a frightened expression.

"I know it's only a million, but that should keep you going for a while. I'm transferring it from my account to yours, against the sale of your stocks, with the usual six-percent interest for the use of my money. You oughtn't to object to that.

"When the price goes high enough, Titus, Farnsworth & Quinn will unload your holdings. Those boys can unload a million shares on a weak market without even shaking it.

"Now, my advice is to get your personal problems and desires out of the way. I want you to begin here with a completely free mind—"

"Look here," said Hale, suspiciously. "You're taking this partnership pretty damned smoothly."

"Well," said Johnson with a humorous expression, "you blackmailed me into it. All I can do is accept the situation gracefully and try to make use of you.

"Incidentally, our prospective victim owns a very presentable yacht. If you'd like one, I know he'll be glad to sell at your price.

"Now, you run along home and get your personal problems settled. I'll phone you every evening. When you're free, I'll spend the evening with you and explain what I've been doing, to give you the proper perspective." He held out his hand. "Goodbye, William. Remember, *don't neglect anything that will make you happy.*"

They shook hands, and Hale left the office, very unsteadily. On the way out he was surprised and pleased to see that a man was putting his name on the door in gold letters under Johnson's. In his daze he didn't think too much about the phenomenal promptness of this bit of decoration.

It was a beauty. The yacht was just what he needed to make him happy.

Chapter VIII

SUCCESS, HALE RATIONALIZED, when it comes so suddenly and brings so much, needs time and thought to be appreciated. He was happy, without question. There was no reason why he shouldn't be.

First he ordered his landlord to knock out two walls of the gymnasium to make a thirty-by-fifty swimming pool.

Then he had himself measured for a complete wardrobe. That should have given him a kick. It did. He found it exhilarating to be able to choose patterns indiscriminately, know-ing that if he disliked any of the finished garments, they could be immediately replaced. He could have gone on buy-ing indefinitely, but it had to end somewhere. By the time he had twenty-five suits, ten hats, a dozen pairs of shoes, and other items in proportion, the process was becoming tedious.

Selecting the first of each article gave him almost the same pleasure he used to get when buying on a forty-a-week budget. Almost, but not quite. He had never at one time owned more than three suits, an overcoat, a topcoat, three hats, and two pairs of shoes. Each additional item had to be chosen with great care, and was very intimate to him in con-sequence. He knew just which shirts, ties, and socks to wear with each suit.

Now he could let his valet choose his outfits, knowing that the precise Hamilton would never let him wear the same combination oftener than once in three weeks. It was inevitable—and Hale vaguely regretted it—that dressing should no longer be the daily adventure it had been. But Hale was able to rationalize that. It was significant that he could think in no strong terms of enjoyment. He merely thought the enormous wardrobe and the valet to manage it were nice.

The apartment house allowed him basement garage space for four more cars. He bought them. He bought a box at the opera, and a mansion on Long Island, and a hunting preserve in Maine, and a saddle horse. The ability to do those things, he felt rather unemotionally, was nice. But he had to make himself gloat over his new possessions; otherwise he was apt to accept them prosaically.

For a while he resisted the idea of hiring a private orches-tra. But then, he thought, that was no attitude for Lucifer's partner. Knowing he would probably tire of the novelty fairly soon, and hampered by a vestigial sense of economy, he hired a conductor and let him assemble an orchestra on a day-to-day basis.

His staff had no doubt been much relieved when he reappeared at the apartment after his forty-eight-hour disappearance, though they were too well-trained to show it. They worked into their routine without apparent effort.

Of course he was happy. The only thing he needed was a yacht, and that, Johnson told him one night, was just a matter of time.

The papers, as Johnson had predicted, came out screaming one day against the sale of aircraft to friendly nations. It was a vicious foreign entanglement and a violation of the isolation policy. Aircraft stocks dropped drastically. Then the government explained everything, and up went the stock prices. But Titus, Farnsworth & Quinn refused to sell.

Johnson explained that strategy. They had listened to the orchestra playing a program of Hale's selection: Sibelius' "Violin Concerto," Beethoven's "Seventh," and De Falla's "Nights in the Gardens of Spain," and they were sitting in a hitherto useless room that Hale had converted—by having the walls painted black with mirrors set into them and strong white lights to shine on the smoke—into a smoking room.

"This manipulator we cleaned," said Johnson complacently, "paid over a million for his yacht. But he made the mistake of selling short. You know we cornered the market, don't you? That means the only place he can buy aircraft stocks is from us, and he has to pay any price we ask. Get the idea? Well, you want a yacht, and he wants aircraft stocks.

"So I offer him, say, a hundred thousand in cash for his boat. He refuses. I offer a hundred and fifty thousand. He knows he can't get that at auction, so he sells. He still needs shares to cover his short sales. Therefore, Titus, Farnsworth & Quinn offer him a hundred and fifty thousand dollars' worth of stocks—or at least whatever we choose to give him for that much money; very little, I assure you. With the profit on your stocks, your yacht should cost you, at the most, fifty thousand dollars."

Hale lit a cigarette—a personal blend, with his initials on the paper. "That's pretty cold-blooded."

"Yes, I suppose so. However, to operate efficiently as Lucifer's partner, you must understand the philosophy of Hell: Obviously its inhabitants are here to suffer. This manipulator served his purpose often in the past, to strip other speculators. Now his role is merely reversed.

"But you must remember," he said, tapping Hale's chest, "except in unusual cases, I never concentrate on tormenting a single person. That would be inefficient. I explained my strategy in forcing this manipulator into bankruptcy: My policy of isolation needed emphasis; the manipulator had to be stripped eventually; and you needed a fortune. If you have been reading the newspapers, you must have seen the consequences of this simple transaction.

"The chronic state of crisis, never quite reaching war, which I have labored incessantly to create, is kept simmering. The world was growing apathetic, but now there is a very gratifying turmoil. Millions of people have been made afraid and unhappy. Others have had their hopes raised. At the proper moment those hopes will be dashed, and they, too, will be unhappy. Thus this small financial operation lays the groundwork of a plan to make an unbelievable number of people suffer—which is our purpose.

"The philosophy of Hell, my boy—and don't forget

this—is that all its inhabitants are here for the purpose of suffering. They deserve to be here, or they'd be elsewhere. Our function is to cause suffering as all-inclusively and with as low a cost per unit as possible.

"That, William, is our business. A tremendous responsibility, I grant you, but we must never let its scope dismay us. We must have our shoulders to the wheel every minute, and never lose sight of our goal, no matter what the setbacks and disappointments. When we realize a huge, intricate plan, we must not let ourselves grow smug. That success must be the incentive for us to push onward, ever onward and upward."

Hale stared at him in amazement.

He soon lost his astonishment, though, and furtively took to avoiding Johnson whenever he could. Sentiment had nothing to do with this. He loved his sense of power too much. He had accepted the philosophy of Hell, and wasted no sympathy on the souls he would be called upon to torment.

In his social moments, Alexander P. Johnson, despite his professional good humor, was fairly likable. But Hale couldn't stomach his habit of bursting into pompous orations at the slightest excuse or none at all.

Hale was happy, undoubtedly. He thoroughly enjoyed having everybody cater to his whims. The feudal lord that lurks in all of us, no matter how highly our social consciences are developed, bloomed to vast proportions in his highly egocentric nature. The ability to buy anything the moment he wanted it would unbalance any man. Hale was no exception. He gave orders recklessly; and, like anybody else in that position, loved the feel of power.

Naturally, there were certain duties, and it wasn't always possible to avoid Johnson. One night Johnson made him join a businessman's club. Hale, with the ordinary man's dislike of booster organizations, joined unwillingly, and only because his partner explained that it was one of his principal sources of information.

Johnson's actions were suspicious. He got an incredible amount of fun out of putting Hale through a ridiculous initiation, which included filling his unfortunate partner's hair with flour paste. By the time Hale had gotten this goo washed out and had returned to his seat, Johnson was getting even more pleasure out of an impassioned, windy, two-hour speech. His short, gross figure strutted about the rostrum, gesturing elaborately. He looked like a radical cartoonist's conception of Capital. In fact, if dollar signs had been stenciled on his clothes, not only would they have seemed fitting; he would probably have been very proud of them.

Hale discovered that he preferred even a slinking, melodramatic Lucifer to this chubby, jovial Satan who perpetually orated on none but the largest and dullest issues. Superficially there was little difference between Johnson and his fellow club members, who used the meetings for rhetoric inviting everybody to get together and push, because nothing could stop us if all worked together instead of against each other.

When Hale was exceptionally unlucky, Johnson tagged along to plays and concerts. He was lousy company. At any moment he ignored stares and hushings to address Hale in a clear, round voice about social, political or economic movements here and abroad. It was maddeningly boring, and Hale stared straight ahead, raging silently, whenever Johnson spoke.

But Johnson had to be used. So, although Hale dreaded being alone with him for so long, he let him invite himself along on the first cruise when title to the yacht was cleared.

Chapter IX

IT WAS A BEAUTY. There were other yachts in the basin, but Hale saw only the long, slim white ship with polished brass shining in the spring sun. Even when Johnson said, "It cost you only forty-six thousand, my boy," Hale scarcely heard him.

"She's mine!" he breathed.

"Feels pretty good, eh?"

That wasn't exactly the word for it. But Hale couldn't

find the word for it, either, so he kept silent. There was no thrill like it. The yacht was just what he needed to make him happy. Even when a sailor handed him down into a sleek launch and they sped toward the gangway, he was grinning vacantly. The ship expanded almost to liner proportions.

"Hundred and eighty feet long," said Johnson.

"Boy!" said Hale.

They climbed. The crew and officers were on deck, saluting sharply.

"Welcome to your ship, sir," said the captain.

Hale gulped and looked around helplessly at Johnson, who was still climbing.

"Where away, sir?"

"What? Oh, I don't know. I hadn't thought—"

The captain smiled tolerant. "Might I suggest, sir, considering the cold weather—"

"Of course," Johnson broke in, panting. "South toward Hatteras for a day, then back. What do you say, William?"

Hale agreed quickly. The crew saluted again and fell out. Hale rested his hands sensuously on the cold, polished rail and watched trunks and suitcases come aboard. For a while the captain and Johnson stood quietly beside him, evidently respecting his thrill of ownership.

Then the captain asked: "Would you care to inspect the ship, sir?"

Everything filtered through Hale's consciousness through a haze of delight. The fact that the ship had Diesel motors, that it was seaworthy enough for a round-the-world cruise, and so on, contributed very little to his enjoyment. The only fact he could comprehend was that the whole beautiful ship was his.

"Not bad, eh?" said Johnson.

CHAPTER IX

And Hale, lingering in his gorgeous stateroom, grinned blindly at his partner, Johnson seemed to have acquired the habit of slapping him on the back and saying: "Feels pretty good, eh, William? And to think it set you back only forty-six thousand dollars!" Somehow it didn't irritate Hale. And even Hamilton's frozen expression showed traces of a sympathetic smile.

The engines throbbed. Hale stood on the bridge happily watching the New York and New Jersey shores slide past. The fixed smile seemed to have become a permanent fixture. In a dazed sort of way he was running over his possessions in his mind. Only recently he had seemed doomed to a forty-a-week job for life—well, perhaps sixty if he behaved himself—an utterly glamourless wife, and all the other trimmings. More recently he had been ill in a flophouse.

But now!

The yacht nosed out of the Narrows into the deep swells—

Down, with a swift rush, into the troughs—

Up, laboriously, over the caps—

He swallowed desperately and hung on. It became impossible. He clutched for support and staggered below. When he told Hamilton to leave the stateroom, he seriously thought he was hiding all outward signs of seasickness. Hamilton got him to the bathroom just in time.

While he lay flat, with his eyes strained wide, he could just barely tolerate the downward rush of the ship. But his eyes ached and his heart raced painfully. When he tried closing his eyes to rest them, his sudden nausea made it the logical moment to think about death. He felt nothing remote and impersonal about the subject just then. If he didn't die of sea-sickness, he was sure a storm would sink the ship, or it would hit a submerged object.

He sat up, sweating, and instantly fell back. His heart was stopping! He was sure of it.

So that was the idea! He cursed. Lucifer probably strutted around the deck, gloating pompously, boasting about the number of people this small coup would affect.

But Johnson was standing quietly at his side. "Do you want the lights on, William?" he asked solicitously.

Hale managed to shake his head. As he did so, several old-fashioned cannon balls that seemed to have gotten loose inside his skull went slamming around it.

"Do you want anything at all—some lemons, perhaps? I understand they're very good for seasickness."

Hale groaned. "No...I don't mind—"

"What is it then, my boy?" Johnson dragged up a chair and plumped fatly into it. "Are you having mental disturbances, too?"

"You know, don't you?" Hale cried. "You did it, damn you—you flabby devil! You tricked me into it! Very neatly, too?"

"Whatever are you talking about, William?"

Hale lay and glowered impotently in the dusk. "You know damned well what I mean. When I was poor, I didn't even think about dying. When I did, there was nothing terrible about the idea. I wouldn't be giving up much—lousy little job, two-by-four home, the subway whenever I wanted to travel—"

Johnson interrupted thoughtfully: "The slave doesn't fear death."

"Right, you slimy double-crosser! Sure, you gave me the

partnership and all that goes with it—except one thing."

"I'm sorry you feel that way, William. The partnership was your idea, you know. You forced me into it. Haven't I kept my part of the bargain?"

"Yes, you have. But the more you gave me, the more I stood to lose. For the first time in my life I have something to live for: money, cars, a horse, and *power*. That's what hurts most." He pulled at Johnson's sleeve. "You can't kid me into thinking it's a long way off yet. I probably won't die tonight; but you'll go on, immortal, and I'll kick off in a few years!"

Johnson put his hands on his knees and looked at Hale for a while. At last he asked gently: "Are you suggesting that I make you immortal, William? Is that it?"

"Huh?" Hale sat up, heedless of the stab of pain in his head. "You mean you could? You would?"

"I have no objection to doing so, if you want it sufficiently, and you've thought of its consequences."

"What do you mean, consequences? It's easy for you to be cool about it. You're not going to die, so you can afford to weigh the advantages and disadvantages, if any."

"But, William, there *are* disadvantages, you know. I have often been able to sense your hostility to me when we attended the theater. Why do you think I'm not interested in those affairs? To me there's no such thing as a new joke or a new plot. As for music, I've heard every old masterpiece a thousand times, and all the new music I find to be merely a slightly different aspect of the old. Times change, new generations arise, but it's always the same in a different guise. I get new problems, but somehow the old methods of solving them still work very efficiently.

"When you've lived as long as I have, business is the

only thing that can interest you. Luckily I still find the business of running Hell extremely fascinating after all these years. That is my only amusement, and I admit it's enough."

Hale answered: "I don't care. I still don't see you giving up your immortality. Anything is better than this horrible fear. I've got too much to lose. I don't want to die!"

"Then you mean you have decided that you want immortality?"

"Yes. If you can like it, I can."

"Very well, partner." Johnson stood up and shook Hale's hand. "Since you want it, it's yours."

"Huh? What do you mean?"

"Just what I said. You're immortal."

"I'm im— Just like that? I mean, don't you *do* anything?"

"That's all. I assure you you're immortal. I admit it may seem odd, from your point of view. But you should realize by now that I work by everyday, matter-of-fact methods."

"Huh, I still don't get it. How does it work?"

"Immortality? By what is commonly regarded as luck. In our cases, a never-ending series of fortunate accidents. Guns pointed at us happen not to go off, or something happens to the gunners. Accidents occur a moment after we are safely out of the way. We happen not to contract fatal illnesses; our systems happen not to age or deteriorate. There is really nothing magical about it."

"Yeah. On the surface."

"Quite so." Johnson smiled through the gloom. "On the surface."

Hale's first demonstration of his immortality was his quick recovery. He could sit up without vertigo. Johnson turned on the lights and resumed his seat. Before Hale could reopen the subject of immortality, he said: "I understand your swimming pool will be completed when we get back. Have you thought of any ceremony in opening it?"

"I've been wondering about that. Just taking a swim doesn't sound so good. There ought to be some kind of blow-out, only the people I used to know wouldn't fit in."

"Don't you know anybody at all?"

"Just about nobody. Of course, I could invite the superintendent and his wife, or the girlfriend I gave the air to. They'd fit in nicely."

"Come now, William. I'm entirely serious. I know I'm not much company for a lonely young man. And you *have* been lonely, haven't you?"

Hale had to realize that that was the fact, despite his lavish possessions. He now knew that that was the reason for his restlessness. He hadn't been seeing anybody but Johnson and his servants.

"Well," Hale admitted, "I was sort of playing around with the idea of inviting Banner. But he'd turn me down cold after the dirty trick I played on him."

"Banner? Oh, yes, the advertising man who gave you the...uh...job. He has a daughter, hasn't he? Why don't you ask them?"

Hale shook his head. "They wouldn't come."

"They might. Ask them to bring their friends. All they can do is snub you. And the daughter—she gets her pictures in the papers quite often. Pretty, isn't she?"

"A pip!"

"I agree. A very appealing girl indeed. If you're interested in meeting her, I believe it's worth the risk of a snub."

"Yeah. I suppose it is."

"Is there anything you want before I go, William?"

"No, thanks. I'll be all right."

Johnson left. Hale lay looking up at the softly illuminated ceiling. Damn it, he thought, there's always something to take the kick out of life, and it's always the reality that does it. Who would have thought that he could get tired of his apartment? Like everyone else he enjoyed elbow room but, except for purely functional reasons, there was no incentive for going from one room to another.

Or take his horse and cars. Riding had degenerated into routine. And now the yacht. He had imagined himself riding around grandly, taking long cruises when he felt like it.

Possibly the papers would have pictures of him and his yacht, and the thought of making other people envious was an added satisfaction. He hadn't thought of the inconveniences.

Damn reality! First he'd been seasick and afraid of death. Both had vanished; but now he realized that, besides having had the zest taken from sailing by his sickness, he had transferred his loneliness from the city to the ship. For the whole weekend he would eat, sleep, look at the water, and listen to Johnson orate. That was reality.

But it all stemmed from his loneliness, he knew. Once he met Gloria and her friends, everything would be all right. There was the kind of girl he'd always wanted to know— glamorous, beautiful—

On the first day of his cruise, he was impatient to be home.

Chapter X

HALE WAS HAPPY, for several reasons. Johnson was away from the city on business. The pool was even better than he'd been able to imagine from blueprints. The floor was covered with soft, electrically warmed rubber tiling; the walls were quartz glass on all sides; enough room had been left on the sides of the pool for tables and lounging chairs, palms, an orchestra stand, and rubber mattresses for those who wanted to sun themselves.

It was swell, he thought. He let his white toweling robe fall open. He felt more aristocratic than a Roman emperor. If he could only continue feeling that way he couldn't fail to impress her.

He hadn't seen anyone but the press photographers yet. The guests were dressing. The fact that for once he wasn't the only person occupying the place gratified him.

Then Banner came in. He was probably sensitive about his shape, which was rather like Alexander P. Johnson's, only taller, for he wore a business suit instead of being dressed for swimming. He strode up combatively. "You Hale?" he demanded.

Hale hesitated. "Yes, Mr. Banner."

"Never recognize you all cleaned up," Banner snapped. He stepped back and glowered at Hale until the latter grew uneasy. Then his face suddenly cleared and he thumped Hale's shoulder approvingly. "You didn't have me fooled for a second. I can spot a winner every time."

"You're not sore at me?" Hale asked incredulously.

"Me sore at you? What for?" Banner looked hurt. "You ought to know me better than that. Any man who'd keep another from rising is a heel. Besides, seeing you make good boosts my own ego. Shows what a good judge of character I am. Of course, I wasn't too happy when you quit. Nobody likes to lose a good man. I kind of thought maybe Gloria and I shouldn't come here. But what the hell, I like you. And, as Johnson says, you don't know too many people. Meeting Gloria's crowd'll perk you up."

"Johnson?"

"Your partner."

"Do you know him?"

"Met him through the Businessmen's Club. By the way—"

Banner's voice became confidential—"remember what you said about marrying my daughter, the time you busted in on me? Still got that idea in your head?"

Hale flushed. "That was just a bluff. All I've seen of her is her pictures—"

"They're nothing like her, Hale! Can't get her skin and personality in halftones, you know." He squeezed Hale's arm. "Don't jump into anything on my say-so. But I'll tell you straight from the shoulder—you're the kind of guy I'd like for a son-in-law. You have guts and you know where you're going. Know what Emerson used to say? 'The world steps aside for the man who knows where he's going.' Smart fellow, that Emerson."

Hale was silent. It was true: while he had been heading straight for his goal, the world *had* stepped aside for him. Now that he had his partnership, he noticed signs of indecision in himself. For instance, he allowed his servants and Johnson to run his affairs practically without argument. Worst of all, he was waiting almost shyly for Gloria Banner.

He straightened his shoulders and tied his robe belt more tightly. He'd look her over, and if he liked her he'd just go after her the way he'd gone after his partnership.

But he wasn't prepared for the effect that she habitually created. When she entered, her concentrated femininity struck him like a shock.

She was of medium size, dark, and beautiful. She had just the right amount of hair. Her robe was tied so as to show the contrast between her white suit and her fine dark skin. Her features were small and finely matched and haughtily confident.

Naturally, the partly anaesthetized Hale didn't analyze

her to that extent. He felt only uncritical, inarticulate admiration, particularly when she stopped and stood, very still and regal, gazing at the pool. The photographers went into action.

"Hi, Gloria!" Banner shouted irreverently.

That shocked Hale. But then, he thought, he couldn't expect her own father to address her the way one should.

"Daddy! Isn't it wonderful?" Hale thought her voice resembled the tone of an exceptionally mellow flute, and that she ran toward them with the grace of a ballerina.

"Mmmm, it's grand! Why can't we have one, daddy?"

Banner turned to Hale for sympathy, jerking his head at her. "My worthless, spendthrift daughter speaking. Look here, loafer, if you'd stop frittering and get yourself a job—any kind, even if it only pays a couple of hundred thousand a year—we could afford one."

She wasn't listening to him. She smiled brilliantly at Hale. "Aren't you the nice man who asked us?" Her voice made Hale feel that they were alone and had known each other since childhood.

"Well, if that isn't ignorant of me!" exclaimed Banner. "Gloria, this is William Hale. The guy I told you about—the one who broke into my office looking like a bum and—"

Hale broke in swiftly: "I've seen a lot of your pictures in the newspapers."

"Oh, they were terrible. They always make me look so *fat!*"

"You, fat? Why, you...you're—" His glottis closed up with emotion.

Neither looked away from the other. Hale was unaware of Banner, until a ponderously uneasy squirming at his side gave way to: "You two don't seem to have much use for me."

Her eyes broke away from Hale, and she said unconvincingly: "Oh, no, daddy! We'd love to have you stay here with us, but we know business comes first and you have to make friends with the newspapermen."

"Yeah," Banner grinned, walking away. "How did I happen to forget that excuse? See you when you're able to notice *me*."

Through all this, Hale had taken his eyes off her face only long enough to glance at her hair, whose top came to the level of his eyes, convincing him that she was the perfect height for him.

Her friends entered loudly. She put on a bathing cap and pulled him to the edge of the pool. "Let's be the first ones in—Billie-willie!"

"Billie-willie?" he asked, slightly embarrassed.

"I can't call you William or Bill," she whispered conspiratorially. "Not when we're alone together. It'll be a secret for just the two of us. You don't mind, do you, Billie-willie?"

He didn't. He felt the pleasant outrage you feel when somebody gives your name an unexpected but intimate twist. He wanted her to call him that every time they were alone, and he wanted to be alone with her a lot.

"No," he whispered back. "I think it's...swell."

She wrinkled her nose at him. The room was filling with chattering people who made enough noise for a movie storm scene. But Gloria had the rare knack of making a man forget that other people were living. She wriggled out of her robe, smiled back at him, and took a perfectly ordinary dive.

That made him feel even better. He knew he was a miserable diver. But, while her eyes were on him, he wasn't afraid of smacking the water with his stomach. As a result he did fairly well, and came up with his face a foot from hers.

They trod water abstractedly. He said her bathing cap gave her face a heart shape, and she said it was a horrid old thing, and he said he'd like anything she wore. They might have gone on this way indefinitely if a man hadn't yelled: "Hey! Got room for us down there, Mr. Hale?"

They came to and swam off slowly, close together, oblivious to the men and girls doing neat dives all around them. The spell of intimacy was somehow unbroken, though the photographers were flashing bulbs with the fury of madmen, and the orchestra broke into a crash of music.

The thin moon was setting when they took a tray of sandwiches and stole off to a deserted corner and sat on an inflated mattress. "Happy?" he said eagerly.

She nodded and sighed. "It must be grand fun, having a swimming pool in your own home."

He watched her take a dainty bite on a sandwich. "It is, when you're here. Otherwise it would be about the same as owning a bathtub."

He had known her for several hours, but meeting her gaze still had a physical shock for him. Her eyes were large, deep, gravely thoughtful, and probably myopic.

He said: "You make everything seem—I don't know how to put it—exciting is the word, I guess. I've never known a girl like you."

"I'm just like any other girl—"

"No, you're not! You have glamour. You're beautiful...and everything."

Her smile was touchingly uncertain. "I like you, too. I don't want you to feel alone any more."

"What do you usually do?" he asked suddenly.

"What? What do you mean?"

"I mean for amusement. Do you like plays and concerts?"

"I do, but the boys I used to go with never seemed to care much for them."

He opened his mouth. *Used* to go with? Did she mean what he hoped she meant?

"I'm afraid I don't know much about music and the theater. I'd love to learn. Would you teach me, Billie-willie?"

He trembled with excitement. "We'll go to plays and concerts and art galleries, and we'll see only the best movies together," he said with a rush of enthusiasm.

"I'd love that. I want to like everything you like—"

He thought happily, all she needs is molding. Her beauty was enough for any man, but she also had intelligence and the desire to learn. All he had to do was teach her to enjoy the things he liked. Then she would be a fit mate for Lucifer's partner—lovely, dainty, and, ultimately, intellectual. Training her would give him the creative joy of the master sculptor.

She did not resist when he put his arm around her.

Who would have thought that he could get tired of his apartment?

Chapter XI

JOHNSON WAS VERY PATIENT. Realizing that Hale was distracted, he did not insist on the co-operation he deserved. In the few times that he succeeded in finding Hale at home and tried to continue his lessons in methods of ruling, he treated Hale with remarkable tact. "If anyone has the right and the power to gain happiness," he said once, "it's you. Don't rush yourself. Think this thing out. If you need any help, ask me for it. Meanwhile, I won't bother you until your mind is free. But, William, I want to impress this on you—anytime you're stuck, just remember what you are."

From then on he kept away entirely, to allow his partner to solve his personal problems. Hale was grateful for his understanding. At the moment he couldn't even think about co-operating with Johnson. He was too absorbed in teaching Gloria to enjoy the arts. He thought she was making progress.

Drinking highballs in a club after a play, he asked: "What did you think of it?"

"I don't know. I didn't like it much." He brightened. "Why?"

"Well, you said the main thing about any kind of literature isn't the premise. Isn't that right?"

"That's right. Any premise is acceptable. Go on."

She lifted her great, serious eyes to his. "But the development must be logical, you said. The girl was in love with a rich man, but she married the poor one because she thought it would be more romantic. I wouldn't be so silly. I'd marry the man I loved. And would you kill yourself like the rich man?"

He recoiled slightly, staring down at her lovely, affectionate face in horror. Kill himself? He couldn't. But she—

"What's wrong, Billie-willie?"

"N-nothing."

She clutched his hand desperately, while he gabbled wildly about anything that came into his mind; anything, that is, but the frightening thought that she had innocently aroused.

She had several little ways that flattered him into thinking that she regarded him as a terrifyingly strong brute, though he had always considered himself more the intellectual type. When walking, she would hold his arm muscle in an awed grasp.

She would beg him to let her handle the wheel of one of the cars, and then gasp that she didn't know how he did it so well, and that she felt so much safer driving with him than with anyone else.

It made him feel equal to anything, even to running Hell as an equal partner. That, he thought, was what a man needed a woman for. The question of her intellectual development would take care of itself.

He was incredibly happy—except for one upsetting thought. This he kept submerged in his subconscious as long as he could, until an accident forced it so emphatically on his mind that he could no longer ignore it.

Frozen in horror, Hale saw the hurtling body falling—falling straight at him!

Chapter XII

HE STRODE ALONG Fifth Avenue. If he hadn't been thinking about Gloria he would probably have enjoyed the warmth of the early spring.

Something reached the rim of his abstracted mind, but did not penetrate. It was a scream from somewhere above him. Then people were shouting all around him, and backing away, gaping up.

The scream from above grew louder. Its agony shocked

him awake. He looked up. A man came hurtling down through the air—a window washer whose strap had broken. He was aimed so perfectly that Hale knew he couldn't escape. But he couldn't move aside. He was numb.

And then a wind blew up—a sudden, fierce wind that slashed along the street without warning. Hale's hat blew off. The turning body grew larger, plummeted straight toward Hale's head. The wind caught it, whipped out the clothes into sails. Its fall broke at an angle without stopping. It splashed ten feet from Hale.

People milled and shouted. Hale stood still. He couldn't get it through his head that he'd escaped. The man had fallen right at him.

When he did understand, he trembled uncontrollably. His knees sagged, and his stomach felt like giving up. Somehow he signaled a taxi and choked out the address of the clipping bureau.

Before, he had not entirely accepted Johnson's assurance of immortality. He couldn't question it now. Anyone else in his place would have been smashed flat. Only that sudden, fierce wind—outwardly there was nothing supernatural about it. But Hale knew better. And the knowledge scared him witless. Not for himself, but—

Johnson eased him into a chair. "Calm down now. You're still suffering from shock, but you'll get over it."

Hale babbled; "He was falling right at me! Then the wind—and he missed me!"

"Naturally," purred Johnson. "I told you something would always happen. It always will."

"But that's what I mean! I'm immortal!"

"Didn't I tell you you were?"

"You don't understand. *I'm* immortal. *She* isn't. She'll grow old and die—"

"Oh, so that's what is bothering you. Why don't you stop jittering and calm down? I had to face that problem many times when I was younger."

"You?"

"Certainly. What's so remarkable about that? I got married occasionally. And every time I fell in love, I had to fight out the problem of whether to make the girl immortal. I resisted the foolish impulse, and let me tell you, was glad every time.

"You get tired of women, same as anything else. After a while it's a great relief to see their skins get wrinkled, their hair grow white, and their pretty teeth fall out. You know the end isn't far off, and you'll be rid of them."

"Stop it!" Hale banged the desk with his fist, then sat back into his chair with his head in his hands.

"I'm sorry," said Johnson. "I didn't know you felt so strongly about her. Well, anyhow, the shock has made you think about what you're going to do. I haven't said anything, of course, but I've felt you haven't been fair to me."

"In what way?" Hale asked hollowly.

"Why, I made you a partner, with equal rights and obligations. But I've been doing all the giving. Not that I'm protesting, understand. You wouldn't be worth much to me while you were mooning around. But eventually it would have to be Gloria or the business, or finding a way to reconcile them.

"I have to leave for Europe soon, and I thought I'd let you manage things in this hemisphere. You can, if you've gotten your personal affairs settled. So the question is, what are you going to do?"

"I don't know," moaned Hale.

"Come now, William. Be sensible. You can give her up, or you can marry her."

"I *couldn't* marry her!"

Johnson spread his white hands. "Then give her up."

"I can't do that, either! I love her!"

Johnson waddled around the desk. "Oh, for goodness' sake! If you can't marry her, give her up. If you can't give her up, marry her. That's logical, isn't it? What else can you do?"

"I don't know."

"William! You must stop being sentimental and selfish. I think I've been as patient as anyone could be, but you do owe the business a certain amount of loyalty, you know. Don't you *want* to marry her?"

Hale nodded. "But I'm immortal, and she isn't. She'll grow old and die—"

"Well, personally, I couldn't imagine a better arrangement."

"I don't want her to die! I want you to make her immortal—"

"*Me*? Why should I? It isn't my problem."

"You won't do it? I thought you wouldn't, you—"

"Now, wait a minute, William. You're my partner, aren't you? Which means you have equal rights and powers."

"You mean *I* could make her immortal? How?"

"The same way I did with you. Settle the question any way you see fit, but please do it soon. I really can't spare much more time away from Europe, and I have a new development in stock-market manipulation to explain to you, when you're in a more receptive mood."

Hale felt around for his hat; then remembered that he had

lost it. He began to stumble out of the office.

"Now, William," Johnson cautioned, "don't rush into this immortality business. It's a serious matter. Give it your careful consideration first—"

"Yeah, sure," Hale muttered. But he scarcely heard Johnson. *He* had the power of giving Gloria immortality!

"The balance of power has been upset. The dictatorships have been taking advantage of the military and psychological weakness of the democracies."

Chapter XIII

THE EVENING NEWSPAPERS had shouted:

1 MIN. 75 MI. GALE
PANICS CITY CROWDS

Nevertheless, the phenomenally balmy weather continued. The papers had a scientific explanation for the unsea-
sonable warmth—something about a high-pressure area.

Anyway, the weather was as fine as if somebody had planned it that way for Hale's express benefit.

But Hale hadn't been able to concentrate on newspapers for several weeks. For him, it was the perfect end to a miserable day. He had dutifully tried to think of reasons why he shouldn't give Gloria Banner immortality. She might grow bored and hate him for it; she might get lonely with nobody but himself and Lucifer for company.

Naturally, these arguments weren't convincing. Though he tried to be fair, he hadn't really meant them to be. He had to picture but one vision to find himself shaken and sweating with a near-hysteria. Johnson's words! Gloria, a withered, toothless, mumbling hag.

He shuddered violently, and drew Gloria to him, dropping his face on her shoulder.

"What is it?" she whispered, running soothing fingers through his hair, in woman's instinctive, mothering gesture.

"I love you so...love you," he half gasped, half sobbed. Floating before his eyes, closed or opened—withered—pursing, mumbling, mouthing gums—

She laughed softly, held him closer. "And that makes you shudder so? Why, dear? You know—you must know by now—that I love you. Is that cause for shuddering?"

"Oh, God, Gloria"—the vision rose and mumbled in his face—"you must stay with me, must—"

Suddenly she stiffened, he could feel her breath catch, and her hand stopped abruptly its tender, stroking motion. "You love me, but—" She writhed from his arms, stood up, and darted away, sobbing, across the penthouse terrace, to stand rigid, with her back against the wall of the house, clenched fist pressed against her lips.

CHAPTER XIII

Hale started after her, but she pushed him away. "No...no...go away!"

"Sweetheart...why? What is it—"

"You love me...but you are ashamed of me! You shuddered when you said it! You are ashamed to love me...you're always trying to change me. You are ashamed of me because I like the things all women like—clothes and parties, movies and just talking about us."

"Oh, my dear, no! You're wrong...so wrong! I don't want to change you, ever! It's the fear that somehow you will *change*, be another, horrid person, not the sweet, small self you are tonight, that worried me.

"I want you and need you, Gloria, now and forevermore, more truly than any man ever wanted and needed a woman before in all the world. I don't want you to change—ever."

Reluctantly, she let him pull her hands from her eyes, and slowly slipped into his arms, looking up at him with moon-silvered face and dark, fearful eyes.

"Really, dearest?"

"Most truly, Gloria. I ask one thing, and make one prayer: that we be ever together, never apart, and never happy apart—you, I, and our love together everlasting; you, I, and our love alike never changing—to eternity!"

He kissed her very gently on each eyelid, and on the lips, and looked down again into her face. Slowly the haunting fear was leaving her moon-darkened eyes; she smiled up tremulously, believing now, and abruptly clung to him, her face buried against his coat, her hair gleaming silver under his fingers.

Thousands of people seemed to be congratulating him all day long. At least half of them, in retrospect, were Johnson and Banner, repeating at set intervals how lucky he was, and she was, and they were.

He never remembered much of the actual ceremony. The quickly installed organ moaned, and featureless faces surmounting elegantly clad bodies were packed into the huge room. He numbly watched Gloria, her father, little flower girls and page boys, and dozens of maids of honor march down the velvet toward him. Even Johnson, at his side, kept a dignified silence.

He had a vague impression of Gloria standing beside him in a flowing white gown. He mumbled something to someone who asked him something. He kissed her. Then sighs, tears, applause, hundreds of handshakes. There was a glass of champagne in his hand. That was gone. He was dancing with her. Eating.

They were whisking through the streets to the yacht basin. Everybody was talking and laughing. Banner was shaking his hand, saying: "Thought you'd get the best of me, huh? Got you right where I want you. Johnson and I thought you'd make a damn fine son-in-law. Had my eye on you all the time."

Johnson said: "Enjoy yourself, William. Neglect nothing that will make you happy. But remember, one week and not a second more. I can't spare you longer than that."

The launch took them back to the pier. Everybody on the dock waved and shouted and screamed. The ship tooted proudly and moved down the river.

Gloria stood on her toes and lifted her mouth toward Hale's "For always, Billie-willie?" she murmured.

"For always, darling," he promised, gently definite. He had given immortality to the girl he loved—they were married for all eternity—and he had never been so happy in his life!

Chapter XIV

THE MOMENT HE ENTERED the office, Johnson sprang out of his chair and strutted forth to greet him, stomach and hand outstretched. "William, my boy! I certainly am glad to see you. You do look fit, I must say. Much better than when you left. Have a nice trip?"

"It was all right."

"Cruising around the Caribbean, was only 'all right'?"

"You yanked us back just when we were getting started."

Johnson soothed: "When things are more settled, you'll be able to take a round-the-world cruise if you want to. But we can't put pleasure before business, William. Right now everything is sizzling at once, and I really must—"

Hale broke in: "I've been thinking about something. Now that I have everything I want, I'd like to spread the cheer around to a few people who treated me decently."

"Anyone in particular?" Johnson asked, untroubled by the interruption.

"The Burkes, the janitors who took care of me. I'd like to make them happy if I can."

"How? Money, I suppose?"

"I guess so. Yeah, sure. That's what they need most."

Johnson pushed a buzzer with one hand, and shoved a pad and pencil toward Hale with the other. "Write the name and address."

When Hale had done so, Johnson handed the sheet to a prim middle-aged secretary who had appeared, and said: "Call up these people and find out where they came from. Get all the information you can squeeze out of them."

"I don't get it," said Hale. "Are we working on the Burkes already?"

"Of course, William. In our line of business, to think is to act. No time wasted; no false motions. You'll find that an excellent slogan to guide you while I'm away. Think a while, naturally; but the principal thing is to act, even if you're wrong."

He hitched his chair closer. "Now I'll explain the situation in Europe. You know that we are responsible for the fact that this country is shipping aircraft to friendly nations. As a result, the balance of power has been upset. The dictatorships had been taking advantage of the military and psychological weakness of the democracies.

"But although the totalitarian nations had based their economies on the production of armaments for several years, America, within a short time, could produce more armaments than all those nations together! You really have no idea of our productive resources. For instance, we produce normally something like twenty-five thousand automobiles per *week*.

"It would require no great effort to convert a large fraction of our plant to the production of tanks and military trucks and supply carriers, and turn out several thousand airplanes per week as well.

"You can see what that would do to the production of the most industrialized of the dictatorships, about which they have been boasting recently—a mere ten thousand planes a *year*!

"Almost without disturbing our national economy, we can mechanize all the democratic armies, feed them, clothe them, and supply them with the world's most efficient weapons, in less time than you could imagine.

"The autocratic nations fully realize that. In any case, their economic systems are practically exhausted. They have been able to arm themselves as much as they have only by creating nearly self-sufficient economies: controlled currency, import restrictions, and so forth.

"If I leave them to themselves, they will go to war, in the hope of achieving a quick victory before American help can count.

"But you understand the philosophy of Hell. My strategy worked with its usual beautiful precision. The autocratic nations are experiencing a first-rate crisis, and the democracies feel rather secure for once. The dictatorships are close to war.

Now, William, tell me what you would do if you were I."

Hale looked thoughtfully at his cigarette lighter. "What would I do? Why"—he lit the cigarette ponderously, giving himself time to think—"I guess I'd try to prevent war."

"Of course." Johnson nodded, pleased. "But for what purpose?"

"To keep the world frightened as long as possible."

"Fine! Admirable! That is exactly what I intend doing. War is often an emotional stimulant, or at least can be given a romantic gloss. I find that fear of war is much more debilitating. So I want to continue piling crisis on crisis, making first one side panicky and then the other.

"Eventually, of course, the world will come to accept war as inevitable, and feel that they want to get it over with. At that point I shall allow war to come. Then the hysterical apathy produced by constant fear will be drowned in the reality of war's horror. That point, however, has not yet been reached."

Johnson lit a cigar. "Right now there is danger of either war or peace breaking out in Europe. The aggressors can't increase their production of munitions. But their economies are based on arms manufacture; if they stop producing them, they will collapse, or be overthrown from below. Obviously, I can't let them go to war, stop producing munitions, or be overthrown. Then what is the solution, William?"

Hale saw none. The dictatorships were trapped. Unless—"No," he said. "They wouldn't do it."

"What wouldn't who do?"

"The democracies wouldn't float a loan and feed them raw materials."

"What makes you so sure?"

CHAPTER XIV

"Why should they? They'd be arming the people they're preparing to fight."

"Ah!" said Johnson smugly. "You haven't examined all the facts. Remember that the dictatorships have defaulted on a lot of debts to the smaller nations, who have had to take goods instead of money in payment. And, furthermore, these debts will be repudiated altogether if the dictatorships are overthrown. Which means that the smaller nations will collapse if the dictatorships do.

"Much as the democracies fear war, they fear a general political upheaval even more. I shall play on that fear. There will be a huge loan to the dictatorships, and all the raw materials they can absorb. Thus the danger of peace will be removed; everybody will be producing munitions madly; and the chronic state of crisis will be kept furiously boiling. Do you agree with me?"

Hale shook his head slowly. "I guess I'll never learn."

"Nonsense, William! It may take you a few years, perhaps even centuries. What of it? We have all eternity before us. Simply remember this."

He tapped on the desk for emphasis. "Our business, let me repeat, is to torment the greatest number of people in the most efficient manner possible. War, or the fear of war, is the greatest mass torment.

"But there are other torments for nations, or classes within nations: unemployment, taxes, unbalanced budgets, business competition, threats of social upheavals, relief slashes, and so on.

"Even though the war crisis is our most absorbing problem at the moment, we must never cease using the smaller torments."

Quite naturally, Hale had been feeling increasingly unsure of himself. His motive in forcing Lucifer to give him a partnerhship had been nothing more satanic than a desire for wealth, luxury, security, and a little power—enough to make him feel important.

He felt inadequate, though, when it came to ruling the world with Lucifer.

"What am I supposed to do while you're gone?" he asked uneasily.

"That depends entirely on you, William. If you want to experiment, I have no objections. After all, your powers are the same as mine. Do anything you want. There is a complete plan for the Western Hemisphere already in operation. If you don't feel equal to constructing a plan of your own, I'd suggest that you let that plan work out and study it in operation. But that's your problem."

"What about paying the office help?"

"The company has funds, and there will be money coming in all the time. The loan for the dictatorships, for example, will net us a very large fee, secretly, of course. We are never at a loss for money. He looked at his wrist watch. "I wish that secretary would hurry. My luggage is at the pier, and my ship leaves at noon."

Hale said, "Those files have me scared."

"No reason why they should. Every month the information in them is reduced to graphs, showing the country's economic, social, and political condition. There are several thousand drawers in the files, but they are mostly cross references, not separate entries.

"Suppose there is a rise in employment. You get in touch with our lobby in the State where it occurs; or in Washington if it's nationwide. You begin a movement for greater taxation of profits, or of pay rolls, or anything that will keep the total national income from increasing. Or you can lower the standard of living, by raising rentals and commodity prices, which will have the same effect—"

At this point the secretary returned and gave Johnson a typed sheet. He told her to wait and waddled toward the door, motioning to Hale. He went with fussy haste to the files marked "W," and under "Wisconsin" he found a "Rockmont" card.

"Nothing here," he said. "But Rockmont is in Douglas County, and so is Superior, which is quite a large town. You see, Mr. Burke is a naturalized citizen, which eliminates him. Mrs. Burke, though, was a Greene before she married, and the Greenes have lived in and around Rockmont for generations."

He flipped rapidly through the cards. "Ah, here it is...Superior. Last entry, two weeks ago: 'Nicholas Perry, dying of lung cancer—' Here, read it yourself."

Hale said doubtfully: "I don't get this. What's Perry got to do with it? Why can't I just give them some of my own money?"

"William!" Johnson cried, shocked. "You don't know what you're saying! We're businessmen, running our business on the most efficient, economical lines possible. We can't simply hand out money every time someone needs it. Remember your old strategy."

"*My* old strategy?"

"Of course. Indirection, William. Make someone else pay. It spreads the misery. Did I give you money because you needed a fortune? Of course not; it wouldn't have been efficient. Indirection always works. Before you abandoned it, weren't you able to hide your motives even from me?"

Hale looked up sharply; Johnson's voice had unduly stressed the last sentence. But the round face was entirely innocent. "Whenever possible, we use the hidden finger to gain our ends. Read the card, William."

Hale read: "Nicholas Perry, lung cancer, one month to live. No relatives. Wisconsin family, three generations. Estate income goes to found cancer research laboratory, approx. $25,000/yr."

Johnson said: "I admit I'm tempted not to let the Burkes have Perry's money. Oh, we'll be able to find a connection between the Perrys and the Greenes, all right. Most of the old families are related in sparsely settled places like that, if they'd take the trouble to search the records. But I have a fondness for poorly capitalized research foundations.

"Perry wants to finance one on twenty-five thousand a year. That would pay for very meager equipment, and a small staff of second-rate technicians. Best of all, if they should miraculously discover a cure for pulmonary cancer, they won't have funds to distribute it, so the profit and possibly the credit would go elsewhere.

"It's a temptation, William. But this is your hemisphere, so, of course, the Burkes come first."

He strutted back to his office, and dictated: "Trace a connection, not illegally remote, between the Perrys of Superior and the Greenes of Rockmont, Wisconsin. Have the legal department inform Nicholas Perry that he has living relatives who have a legitimate claim on the estate. If he dies before you can do so, contest the will. That's all."

He turned to Hale. "If Perry leaves the fortune to the Burkes, the inheritance tax will cut the income to about ten or fifteen thousand. Think that's enough?"

"Plenty," replied Hale distractedly. A vague sort of nervousness had been troubling him more and more. Though he tried to act normal, he stood fidgeting behind his chair, glancing longingly at the door.

Johnson watched him curiously, but continued: "If Perry dies before we can reach him, the best settlement we can make will probably be an equal division of the estate between the Burkes and the laboratory. That would hamstring the laboratory effectively enough to suit even me. In any case you can leave the matter, including collection of our fee, to our legal department. By the way, you of course realize that neither they nor any of our other subordinates know who we really are. I really must be going now."

Though he wanted desperately to be home, Hale asked: "Want me to drive you to the pier?"

"No, thank you, William." Johnson was performing the major task of getting into his overcoat. To reach around to find the armholes made him puff and turn red.

He placed a derby squarely on his innocent-looking white head, and teased: "I appreciate your offer, but you don't want to stay away from your bride too long, do you?"

Hale at once understood what was the matter with him. His desire to go home had become an overwhelming fixation.

He rationalized that, since he had been married, he had not been away from his wife for more than a few minutes at a time. So it was natural for him to want to get back to her.

But that didn't explain his preposterous unhappiness at being separated from her. Going down in the elevator he could think of nothing else.

Johnson got into a taxi with elephantine exertion. He said: "Goodbye, William. Do whatever you think best in the way of supervision of the business. You'll hear from me at intervals, and I'll be back in a few months. But remember this: "*Anything you do, no matter what it is, will increase the misery and torments of the people, because that is how Hell is constructed.*"

"Yeah," mumbled Hale unhearingly. "I get it. Goodbye."

Even before the taxi started, he was sprinting to his roadster. Only when he was racing recklessly uptown did he think of a question he had meant to ask Johnson. But he told himself it wasn't important. What difference did it make how long Johnson and Banner had known each other? What of it if Johnson hadn't mentioned it? There was no reason why he should.

Long before he'd started on his campaign to blackmail Lucifer, Hale had seen Gloria's picture in the papers, and had put marriage to her on his list of objectives. So there couldn't be any connection between his marriage and Johnson.

He could still have caught Johnson at the pier, but he didn't think it was necessary. The truth was that even the swift elevator was too slow in bringing him to Gloria. He couldn't wait to take her in his arms.

Chapter XV

HE HESITATED a long time before writing. Then, rather than dictate the letter to his secretary, he borrowed a type-writer and wrote it himself.

Dear Johnson:
I seem to have put myself into a little difficulty.
Maybe you can help me.

He stopped there, his eyes straying to Gloria. She was sitting erect and knitting a sweater with great concentration. Tenderly he watched the smooth skin between her eyes pucker as she solved an intricate problem of knitting, and then relax placidly. It amused her now, being at his office, he thought. Later she mightn't find it so nice.

The night Gloria and I got engaged, I was feeling pretty romantic, naturally, and I said something about us that I guess I didn't phrase properly. Now it seems to have taken hold like a spell of some kind.

I said something to the effect that we'd never be happy apart. Offhand you would think that would imply only a sort of negative unhappiness. But it isn't like that. When we're separated, we suffer miserably. We feel empty, lost, filled with the most intense psychological pain. We want to be together the next possible instant, no matter how difficult or inconvenient getting together would be.

He reread the last sentences, feeling naked at exposing his emotions so completely to Johnson. But this was no time for stoicism. He went on:

I know it was my fault. I should have been more careful, though I didn't know I was casting a spell, and I had no idea our spells were so damned literal. I should have said something to the effect that we'd be happier together than apart. Tell me how to modify the terms of the spell so it will have that effect.

CHAPTER XV

Please answer immediately, air mail, special delivery. I've done all I can to lift the spell, but nothing seems to work. The situation is becoming most uncomfortable.

"Unbearable" would have been closer to the truth, but he sent the letter as it was.

"Come on, darling. Let's go."

"I thought you had a lot of work."

"Not much," he evaded. "It's finished."

It was or it wasn't; he didn't know which. Johnson would certainly have found plenty to do, moving this or that pawn or setting in motion some vast project that would affect the lives of millions of people.

On the few mornings when he came to the office—more out of desperation for something to do than from any taste for diabolical plotting—his secretary brought in reports, clippings, and graphs, and stood around waiting for him to say something. He never could think of anything intelligent. Yet he could see Johnson's plan move to its climax.

The country was divided into three factions: True isolationists, who wanted no European entanglements of any kind; democratic sympathizers, who wanted intervention against the aggressors; and admirers of the dictatorships, who were split into two bodies—a very small group of advocates of intervention on the side of the aggressors, and a larger group who disguised their sympathies behind pleas for isolation.

He could see that, by lobbies, whispering campaigns, and inspired articles. Johnson would keep the three-cornered fight stirred up until every element of torment had been wrung from it, before allowing it to be settled by an actual struggle for power.

The plan seemed overwhelmingly huge and detailed to Hale. It made him feel baffled and frustrated. Johnson would always know what to do. He could pick up the telephone, and the next morning armies would or would not march, millions of people would or would not eat, anything might or might not happen, depending on which pawn he moved.

It was like finding the correct switch out of millions. Johnson could reach out negligently and find it; Hale would have to throw most of them before anything would happen. The point was, he wasn't Lucifer.

In short, he felt the way you would feel if your job were to cause the most misery to the most people in the most efficient manner possible.

He accepted the philosophy of Hell. He had to, seeing the minute amount of happiness and the cosmic amount of pain and torment in the world, and hence being less subject to qualms than unrealistic outsiders.

He wanted to do his job of running the hemisphere properly, but he couldn't.

Experimentally he could goad one pawn to sudden success, or harry another to destruction. But he would have to ignore everything else while he did it, like an inexperienced corporation sending all its salesmen to grab one small order.

"Come on, Gloria!" he cried. "Let's get out of here before I go nuts!"

"Just let me finish this line," she said, and began knitting with frantic haste.

"Oh, please—"

"It'll take me only a second." She dropped a stitch. "Oh, darn!" When he stepped forward angrily: "Just this line, Billie-willie—"

CHAPTER XV

He snatched it away; the next instant he was sorry. He pulled her to her feet and kissed her. "I'm sorry, darling. I'm getting jittery." She smiled forgivingly. "Where do you want to go?" he asked.

She squeezed his arm. "I don't care, I'm happy just being with you."

Yeah, he thought dejectedly, what a spell he'd laid! The idea had been all right, but he should have defined his terms more fully. They certainly weren't happy apart. But that didn't mean that they were happy together.

"Oh, nuts!" he hissed. Who could have figured out in advance how that idiotically literal spell would work out?

She was staring at him, her eyes brimming. "What's the matter now?" he demanded.

"You didn't have to say what you did. I *do* like being with you, even if we don't do anything."

"I was thinking of something else—business."

You bet she liked being with him, Hale thought. Anything was better than having that incredibly painful longing gnaw at them. They couldn't brush their teeth separately without feeling depressed and almost frantic at a few minutes' separation. So, rather than suffer that horror, he took her wherever he went.

But he couldn't bear staying home with her any more than he could help. She would knit and talk about subjects they had exhausted long before, and grow resentful if he read or listened to phonograph records. Or, from boredom, she might call up her friends for a party.

Normally he would have been able to escape into another room, but his damned spell wouldn't allow him to, no matter how much he hated the noise of silly chatter and dance music.

"Let's go to a movie," he said.

"Oh, darling! There's a cute picture at the State, and they have vaudeville. Don't you love vaudeville?"

"Yeah," he muttered. There was a French film at the Playhouse that he had been conniving to see. But Gloria didn't understand French and refused to read subtitles, and, anyhow, she disliked foreign pictures to the point of tears if he tried to force her into going. He couldn't even sneak off by himself to see it. They'd never be happy apart.

He slammed the office door loudly enough to startle the staff. It was the first time he had seen them look up from their work. Oddly, that made him feel better.

For several days he avoided the office. They got up late, dressed and ate quickly, and left the apartment. He could have used his cars, or the yacht, or his recently acquired airplane, to escape the dread Johnson's desk aroused in him. But swift, aimless travel for its own sake had ceased to be entertaining.

He began to prefer walking. He liked the Haroun-al-Raschid feeling that mixing with his subjects, unbeknownst to them, gave him. But—Gloria was not an athletic girl. She preferred high heels to walking shoes, and after ten blocks complained until he called a taxi. Nor could he leave her and walk alone. They'd never be happy apart.

Gloria did let him take her to a serious play. Considering that he had promised not to try to change her, he thought he had done pretty well. It was a great change from movies, musicals and farces, and he enjoyed it. But when they left, Gloria was sullen.

"What's the trouble?" he asked.

She thrust out her chin. "I don't know much about plays, but—"

"—but you know what you like," he finished for her.

"Yes."

He lit a cigarette and asked: "What didn't you like about it?"

"I don't like that deep stuff. What have I got to do with the Irish revolution? I like plays—"

"—that remind you of us. Isn't that right?"

She looked hurt. "You never let me finish—"

He wanted to tell her that she didn't have to, but, no matter how much she annoyed him at times, his love for her kept his tongue in cheek. He said: "Don't you ever get tired of that subject? It isn't inexhaustible."

"It is to me. Love—"

"I know. Love is a woman's whole life." He put his hands on her shoulders. "I don't want to hurt you, darling, but I honestly don't think we're important enough to occupy your whole mind for the length of time you're going to live."

She pressed her fist against her face to keep from crying in the street. "I think we are, Billie-willie."

"Oh, please!" he cried, rebelling for the first time. "I can't stand that idiotic name! Can't you call me Bill or Will or William?"

The fist refused to function as a dam any longer. She dived into the car and curled up in a corner, crying furiously. All the way home he had to protest that his nerves were touchy and that he really loved the nickname, and her, and the inexhaustible subject of themselves.

He wished Johnson would hurry his reply to the letter. Johnson would know how to fix things. It wouldn't be so bad if he could only have some time to himself. Like most people, Gloria was good enough company when taken in reasonably small doses. But twenty-four hours a day, every day, would wear anybody's company thin. If only Johnson would deliver him from her damned bridge parties, her shopping excursions, and the afternoon teas she was going in for! He didn't object to them, for her. But, hell, she might show a little consideration for him.

Every man settling into marriage routine has to make some sacrifice of bachelor privileges. But nobody in history ever had to contend with as much as Hale.

Chapter XVI

A CALL FROM THE CLIPPING BUREAU brought him down in a hurry. With Gloria hanging on his arm he burst into his private office, ripped open the letter, and frenziedly read it without stopping to sit down.

Dully he heard Gloria ask: "What's wrong, Billie-willie?"

He collapsed into his chair and read the letter again. But nothing in it had changed:

Dear William:

I regret having to inform you that nothing can be done to modify or ameliorate your unfortunate spell. If you will recall our conversations on the subject, I specifically advised you not to be hasty. In view of their literal nature, such things must not be undertaken without considerable thought.

You must regard what you choose to call "spells" as a form of chemical action. The analogy is not exact, but it will convey the idea. Consider your power as a sort of catalyst, which induces an irreversible reaction in your subject. This action cannot be halted, modified, or reversed. It can progress but one way, and then only until all the terms of the "spell" are completely satisfied.

In the future, William, I can only ask you to be more cautious in employing your catalytic power. For the present I must admit myself as powerless as yourself, and can only offer my deepest sympathy.

Please do not let your unfortunate situation dishearten you. Though we generally live to regret our romantic outbursts of emotion, they also have their pleasant aspects. If you will concentrate on your wife's charmingly affectionate nature, and the undeniable gratification of an eternal love, I believe you can learn to tolerate the smaller inconveniences.

Hale stared blindly at the letter. He was tied to her and her stupid little feminine amusements forever, and nothing could be done to correct his insane blunder.

"Is it very bad news, Billie-willie?"

Billie-willie—Billie-willie—

He was standing before her with his right fist cocked, and she was recoiling in startled terror from the threat. It shocked him almost as much as it did her. He poured out apologies and tried to take her in his arms. It got him nowhere.

His mind was quite clear, though that didn't make him hate himself any the less. He hated that beautiful, imbecilic face; but he also loved it so that the thought of marring a line of it horrified him. He hated her eternal presence—the swift clatter of her heels, her meaningless soprano chatter, her enormous cowlike eyes—but he also loved her for these things. That, he thought, had been part of his spell.

He'd hog-tied himself beautifully. He couldn't get away from her; loving her as he did, he couldn't have the satisfaction of slapping her down when she drove him frantic, or at least cowing her into not calling him "Billie-willie"; and she'd never change.

That had been part of the spell, too. Of course, she had no doubt had some ability to learn at the time the spell was cast. Did that mean that she still had that ability, since she was supposed to be the same, or did it mean that she couldn't learn because learning would mean changing her nature?

It was a nice paradox; the kind that Hale had once enjoyed teasing his brain with. But he didn't feel much like logical riddles just then. Time would tell about Gloria, and meanwhile there was more to Johnson's letter. He mumbled, "I'm sorry," and sat down.

Since there is nothing to be gained by further

dwelling on that subject, permit me to go on to another matter. Our plans for a loan, through the bank we control, to the dictatorships, and the ceding to them of colonies that produce vital raw materials, are progressing splendidly.

You already know that America's aid to the democracies, may, unless counteracted, have the undesirable effect of forcing the aggressors into war, economic paralysis, or revolution. In Washington a movement will shortly arise to fortify certain Pacific islands. The primary purpose of this is to create another crisis between the isolationist and interventionist camps, but it will have the secondary effect of diverting armaments to some extent from the European democracies.

Should the movement succeed, it would be a serious blow to the aggressor bloc. At present their energies are concentrated on isolating a single important colonial empire—the one we were discussing the day before I left. The western trade and military routes of this empire can already be shut off instantly. The only route left open to defend it is through the Pacific.

If America fortifies these Pacific islands, the empire would no longer be isolated, and the autocracies would be compelled to fight a defensive as well as an offensive war, which they would inevitably lose.

Consequently, I want to direct a powerful opposition against Pacific island fortification. I have made certain that the movement for creating these bases is strong enough not to give up without a battle; on the other hand you must not arouse enough opposition to defeat the motion entirely. Our purpose is to draw out the struggle indefinitely, to hold up fortification and the production of munitions, thus diverting armaments from the democracies, while giving them the false hope that they are going to be supplied very shortly, and keeping the dictatorships aware of the threat of Pacific fortification, which at any moment might become an actuality.

If you feel uncertain about the method of undertaking this task, call me on the overseas telephone, at the bank's number that you will find on the letterhead. In the event of my being elsewhere at the moment, the bank will arrange a telephone connection between us. I should prefer, however, that you solve the problem yourself, as a concrete example of ruling.

Go ahead, Hale, he thought bitterly, go on and rule. You're Lucifer's partner; you have all the power. What if you do bungle? How much worse can you wreck anybody's life than you have your own and Gloria's? That was all he could think of. She was huddled in her chair, sobbing dismally.

Why was he making her unhappy? It wasn't her fault. It was his own idiotically romantic haste to win her, his thoughtless, ignorant way of casting an irrevocable spell. He couldn't pass the guilt to her, as he had tried like a coward to do.

Her repressed sobbing grew to an accusing wail. "I know what it is! You don't love me anymore, Billie-willie!"

"Darling," he whispered humbly, "I didn't mean it. My

nerves got the better of me. It won't happen again, because I really do love you—" And so forth. It was as true as it was false. He loved her as much as he hated always having to be with her. At least, he was pleasantly surprised to observe, he had restrained his twinge of revulsion at the use of his nick-name.

Chapter XVII

BANNER SHOOK HIS HEAD. "I don't understand what you're driving at, son. Either you've got a terrific grudge against the government, or you're getting kind of hysterical, the way you've been acting up. That's why I came up here to your place."

Hale looked at his cigarette and said nothing. To an outsider he must have seemed rather jittery, making impassioned speeches at all the businessmen's associations that he could get entrance to, haranguing them to get together in opposing fortifications and rearmament, to send telegrams to Washington, to demand action from newspapers.

"Tell me what it is, Bill," Banner pleaded, his voice paternally troubled. "None of us like the idea of spending billions on arms, but you don't see us acting like nuts."

"Daddy!" Gloria protested.

"Well, maybe that is putting it a little strongly. But you *haven't* been acting like a normal human being. This rearmament business can't mean all that to you." He hesitated; then, craftily: "Unless you've got some deal up your sleeve and won't tell your father-in-law."

"I just don't like it," muttered Hale evasively.

"Oh, cut it out! I'm not a kid. You don't just not like a thing and spend all your time making speeches against it to anyone who'll listen. What's your angle? If you don't want to tell me, say so." He added unconvincingly: "I don't mind."

When he saw that no explanation was coming. Banner turned to Gloria. "Mind getting my pipe and pouch? They're in my topcoat."

Hale and Gloria both started and went pale. She glanced appealingly at him as she half rose uncertainly out of her chair.

"I'll go with you, Gloria!" Hale cried, unconsciously loud. "I left something in my coat pocket, too."

The color came back to her face. They left the room together. The longer they were married, it seemed to Hale, the more confining the spell became. Neither spoke until they returned. Banner complained: "I don't know what's got into you, Bill. Gloria could have brought whatever you left in your coat. Don't you two see enough of each other all day?"

Gloria collapsed into a chair, and Hale clenched his jaws to keep from shouting.

Hale lay awake, staring at the shaded bulb and hating himself. The faint light didn't disturb him; on the contrary, it gave him a sense of security. Had either of them awakened and found it too dark to see the other, there would have been a small panic until the light could be clicked on.

If he could only make a break—run away, kill himself or her, anything! But that, of course, was impossible. Being away from her was worse than death; and anyhow they were immortal.

Immortal! Lord, no, he prayed, let it not be that; not living in hopeless, dismal proximity forever and ever, until the end of time!

His cruelty to her was cowardice; he lacked the courage to assume responsibility for his own incompetence. From then on, he swore, he would be gentle and considerate with her, to ease the suffering he had caused her.

But he knew he wouldn't because he couldn't. As long as he allowed himself to brood and writhe, it was natural that he should ignore her presence when he could, lash out at her when he was irritated, and perhaps even strike her. He would torture himself by tormenting her, but he would make her suffer more, so that he would feel better by contrast.

He cursed himself for thinking such thoughts. But when he crushed that obsession back into his subconsciousness, another rose to torment him. What was the point in being Lucifer's partner, if he couldn't learn to use his power? He was faced with a problem that, he knew, Johnson considered pitifully simple. Oppose Pacific island fortification.

Yeah? How. Go ahead and oppose. He had tried as hard

as he could, and was getting nowhere, because he didn't know how to use Johnson's methods of moving the right pawn and waiting with perfect and justified confidence for the results. Of course, he could buy up all the newspapers in the country. That ought to work.

But there was Johnson's fat face grinning sardonically at him. "I wouldn't have to spend a cent," he taunted. "I'd just make a telephone call. See? Not even two calls."

"Damn you!" Hale's mind screamed. "I'm not licked yet, you soft white devil! I'll find a way!"

"Yeah?" Johnson smirked. "How?"

"I'll make a telephone call."

One telephone call—but to whom? Hale didn't know. He had proved himself a failure. He couldn't make a simple telephone call.

Chapter XVIII

GLORIA SAT IN HER EASY-CHAIR knitting. You may think that knitting needles are silent. Hale found they weren't. They have a metallic click, shrill enough to make itself heard over every other sound. That is bad enough, but occasionally they halt while the knitter picks up a dropped stitch, and you grit your teeth and wait for the deadly *click, click, click* to resume.

Hale knew he was getting neurotic. He detested himself

for his weakness, but saw no way of correcting it. Who, in his predicament, wouldn't feel helpless and incompetent? From behind that desk, Johnson had been able to draw in all the complex threads of greed, hope, ambition, and fear, and by pulling the correct thread to rule the world.

Out in the loft were the baffling index cabinets, waiting passively to give up their universal knowledge. But Hale cringed at the thought of approaching them.

All around the private office were tall, gloomy book-shelves filled with volumes on law, medicine, science, gov-ernment, economics, statistics; revolutionary, counter-revo-lutionary, and status-quo propaganda; lists of pressure groups, with their methods and aims and weaknesses; ency-clopedias, year-books—

Everything was there for him—everything that is, but skill and understanding.

He forced his mind to attack the problem calmly, one thing at a time. "Right now the men in power are strong interventionists, with all the prestige of office and the means of propaganda at their disposal. On my side, the iso-lationists are divided and spread all over the country. The idea is to get all these scattered isolationists together."

The telephone rang. "Mr. William Hale?"

"Yeah."

"Transatlantic telephone call. Will you please stay near your telephone until we connect your party? Thank you."

It was Johnson, of course, perhaps calling to jeer at him.

"Hello. Hale speaking."

"Hello, William!" Johnson's cheerful, very human voice responded. "I must say it's certainly fine to hear you. How are you?"

"You know how I am," Hale snapped, and was instantly sorry.

For Johnson said: "Oh, I'm sorry, William. I wish I could do something to make you less miserable." The voice brightened. "At any rate, I've given you something to take your mind off yourself. You know I could have done the job myself without much trouble, but it was you I was worried about. How are you progressing?"

"Lousy."

"I know. I'm sorry to hear it. But cheer up; it doesn't matter very much. The main thing is getting your mind off your personal worries, and practicing up a bit in practical ruling. Do you know why you're not progressing, William?"

"Yeah. I'm just a flop, that's all. Any time you want to unload me, go ahead. I can't even run my own life right."

"Oh, come, William! I can't very well do that. An efficient businessman lives up to his word. What confidence would you have in me if I broke our contract simply because you don't know all I know? No, William. When I make a contract, I regard it as an unbreakable obligation, just as any other responsible businessman—"

"O.K.," Hale broke in to stop the flow of words. "I get you."

"Splendid. I want us to understand each other. Now, putting aside the notion that you are a failure, let us consider why you are not progressing. You remember the letter I wrote you, don't you?"

"Yeah."

"Did you read it carefully? I think you missed something. You see, William, I've had daily reports of your activities sent here, so I could correct your mistakes whenever necessary. I don't want you to feel hurt or think I'm snooping.

Nothing of the sort. Any efficient businessman takes pains to see that his associates are doing their jobs as well as possible, for the sake of the business.

"The point you missed is that I didn't ask you to *create* opposition. That is unnecessary, because it already exists. All that is lacking is centralization and direction, plus some other vital element I want you to discover for yourself."

Hale squirmed on his chair. "I tried to get the businessmen's leagues to fight, because I knew they were already opposed—"

"The idea was correct," Johnson soothed, "but the application wasn't. To weld the businessmen's leagues into a single organization would require *creating* the entire organization; and that isn't worth the trouble, even if it were in line with my policies. An effective organization, with all the necessary contacts, already exists.

"Why don't you look in my files, William? If you're going to oppose the government, why don't you employ an organization that is either part of the government or very close to it?"

"You mean...lobbies? But they're doing all they can."

"Certainly," the smooth, confident voice replied. "And it's evident that they aren't succeeding too well. Why? Obviously, some important part of their equipment is lacking. Your task is to supply that equipment, but remember...indirection and the cheapest, swiftest means!

"Another point...I must hurry; our time is almost up. Under no circumstances should you compromise an organization that might be useful in the future.

Choose a basis for opposition that will not arouse sufficient criticism to destroy your ally.

America, obviously, must be defended; therefore, you

can't oppose on contrary grounds. That would be treason. So you must oppose for a convincing yet patriotic reason—"

The operator's voice interrupted: "Your three minutes are over, sir."

"Yes, yes. Well, Goodbye, William. Try to forget your personal worries, and give my love to Gloria—"

The telephone went dead. Hale stood up. It was just like Johnson, damn him—three times and no more; efficiency, economy!

Gloria looked up inquiringly. "Was that Mr. Johnson, dear?"

"Yes. He sends his love to you."

Gloria flushed with pleasure. Hale, feeling anything but joyful, stood with his hand on the doorknob. He couldn't go into the outer office without her, but he didn't like to disturb her. Forget his troubles—yeah!

"Gloria," he said, "do you mind coming with me?"

"Just this line, Billie-willie; only a minute!"

Billie-willie—and always a line to be finished.

"Sweetheart," he hissed dangerously, "you can finish it later."

"I'll be finished in a sec—"

He dragged her hands from the needles as gently as his rage would allow and pulled her after him. He could have gone without her, but it would have made him as frantic as she would have been.

He thought he'd have to try simply walking out more often when he wanted her to come; as he had by far the stronger personality, he ought to be able to stand the resulting agony longer than she could.

If she could learn anything, she could learn to stop that damned knitting when he wanted to go somewhere.

He studied the filing cabinets while Gloria stood by, annoyed and bored. There was a whole drawer devoted to lobbies: lobbies having to do with airports, boycotts, civil liberties, defense, education, embargoes, exports, farming, flood control, government spending, imports, isolation, liquor, merchant marine, naval construction, prohibition, public utilities, railroads, religion, roads, subsidies, tariffs, taxes—

Hale pondered over the "Isolation" envelope. Were the isolationists really his natural allies? He tried to imitate Johnson's reasoning. In the face of savage aggression all over the world, they protested that America was in no danger.

Many were sincere, but many were patently admirers of the dictatorships, and used isolation merely to advance the interests of these predatory governments.

And there were enough extreme reactionaries, extreme radicals, screwballs, revivalists, impartial manufacturers who sold to both sides and looked for a solvent middle, and agents of foreign governments to discredit the whole movement.

Nope, thought Hale, not the isolationists. Then who? Well, that brought up the question of a popular basis for hamstringing fortification without completely squashing it.

How do you hamstring legislation? You can fight to have it thrown out altogether, or filibuster, or whittle it down so outrageously that the other side will repudiate it in that form.

And there it was, staring Hale in the face. In principle, agree with the need for fortification; in practice, cut down the appropriations on grounds of economy. Neither side will give in without a long, bitter fight, with equal logic and good faith on both sides.

Hale felt his chest expand; he even smiled brilliantly at Gloria. Economy.

There it was: "Economy Lobby" with all the details of adherents, connections, and resources. "Reason for ineffectiveness: Lack of funds."

That stopped him for a while. He couldn't give them money, or solicit for them openly. That would make him conspicuous, and involve expense, one of Johnson's greatest horrors.

He flipped through the entries to their resources. Small loans, small gifts, nothing that would pay for a really big campaign, with broadcasts and printing. Hold it!

"Donation 10,000 shares common stock, Strike Gold Mining Corp., par value $1,000,000; market value, nil. Satiric gift of T. Sloan Blackett, economy legislation foe and ardent government supporter. See: Strike Gold Mining Corp."

Hale shoved back the drawer and moved down to the one marked "STO-STR."

"Strike Gold Mining Corp., near Curtis, Mont, founded ... date of incorporation ... officers ... capitalization ... Mine abandoned, workable ore exhausted. Geologic survey indicates small deposit of tungsten beneath present mine level, rare in United States and never in commercial quantities, thus unlooked for by company geologists and unknown to officers."

Hale grabbed Gloria and shocked her with a kiss. When she tried to prolong the unexpected favor, he dragged her into the private office. Her face fell when he snatched at the telephone instead of at her.

He called Titus, Farnsworth & Quinn. When a suave

voice said, "Titus speaking," he replied cheerfully: "Hello, Titus, Johnson & Hale. Buy up a controlling interest in Strike Gold Mining, on margin, of course, and at the lowest possible price."

Wounded, Titus said: "You don't have to tell me that, Mr. Hale. But I don't seem to remember this Strike company. Mind waiting a minute while I look it up?" Silence, then: "Are you sure you've got the right name? Strike hasn't been on the board for years."

"Yep. Strike Gold Mining Corporation."

"Well, I guess you know what you're doing. But that mine isn't worth a dime. What's up, Mr. Hale?"

"A new engineering report. Get in on the ground floor if you want to, as long as you throw your votes my way. Send some reputable engineer out to the property. Got that?"

"Yes."

"Tell him to look for tungsten! He won't believe it, but he'll find out for himself. Send word out to the newspapers. And then, Titus, I don't have to tell you what to do. Just remember the tungsten deposit'll give out in a short while. Understand? Now let's see a quick job."

"Yes, sir, I understand all right. Thanks for the tip, Mr. Hale. Goodbye."

That was the way to forget his troubles. Hale slapped the desk and grinned. How's that, Johnson?

Chapter XIX

FOR A WHILE Hale behaved like any creative artist whose work is just beginning to arouse interest. He demanded hourly reports from Titus, Farnsworth & Quinn, and bought every edition of every newspaper in the city.

Though outwardly he tried to be casual and businesslike, like Johnson, he got the most intense pleasure out of watching each step follow the last.

It wasn't first-page stuff, of course, but it had its results.

Hale began to understand Johnson's reliance on human nature to carry through the plans he started.

Hale didn't have to nurse his stock up; there were plenty of men, with little personal interest in it, to do that for him.

The reason was that tungsten was one of the few metals America had to import. It wasn't as important as manganese or nickel; but the financial reporters felt that an American tungsten mine was something to be encouraged, and succeeded in making the investors feel the same way.

The mechanics of the transaction interested him less. His brokers had privately bought shares from the large holders for twenty cents to a dollar ten. From there the stock bloomed to 53 1/8, but Hale and his brokers had slid out at 47.

Nor, still following Johnson's thought processes, was he much interested in the eventual collapse of the stock back to nothing, or in the fact that he had incidentally doubled his fortune.

What was important was that the economy lobby had sold out its holdings near the top, and now could make itself felt in Congress. T. Sloan Blackett, the pump-priming advocate, was busily kicking himself for his nose-thumbing gesture at the lobby, which had given it all the money it needed.

Which meant that Hale was finally a full-fledged partner! By hard work and self-confidence he could—almost—forget the degrading terms of his marriage.

It did occur to him, to his mild annoyance, that Johnson wouldn't spend all his time watching one plan develop, but would go on to another. So Hale tried to concoct another.

The press empire of old Bispham had been teetering on the edge of bankruptcy for some time, and the publisher had been liquidating his fantastic collection of art treasures to keep solvent.

CHAPTER XIX

Hale knew that, unless he got a good-sized piece of cash within a few weeks, at least half his papers would disappear or be lost to his control. Hale knew that Johnson had a professional fondness for Bispham.

Besides his papers' editorial policy of appealing to their readers' most primitive and irrational prejudices, they carried the magnificent Sunday magazine sections full of cabalistic lore, astrology, numerology, and superstition generally.

Superstition, as Johnson had explained, was something to be encouraged. The more irrationally people acted, the more often and surely they would be disappointed, and hence the more efficiently Johnson and Hale would have done their jobs.

So Hale tackled the problem of keeping Bispham afloat. He mustn't do it too successfully; just enough to keep the old scoundrel hanging on in eternal fear of the dissolution of his carefully constructed empire. That would make him unhappy, you see, while affording him the opportunity of contributing to the unhappiness of millions of others.

Among the art treasures, according to Johnson's files, was an alleged Titian that was, unbeknownst to its owner, a phony.

Now, if Hale could only find some newly rich and ostentatious person to take it off Bispham's hands at a good round price—say $500,000—and present it to some museum— Bispham would be tided over, the museum would have the exquisite disappointment of looking its gift horse in the mouth, and the rich person would suffer the mortification of being publicly proclaimed a Grade A sucker. Thus everybody would be made suitably unhappy.

But where would Hale find his sucker, and how would he insinuate the idea into his skull?

While he pondered these questions, he amused himself by wandering among his subjects in the manner ascribed to Haroun the Blessed, but actually practiced, not by that cautious caliph, but by Balibars the Tartar, Sultan of Egypt. As he was not compelled to walk, he enjoyed walking; nor could Gloria stop him. He refused to give up this small pleasure, and of course, she had to go along.

He could even enjoy walking in the spring warmth along Sixth Avenue. He could still pity the unemployed, shuffling like wraiths past the employment agencies.

But in his buoyant mood his pity was more remote than it had formerly been; the sort of impersonal sympathy you feel when you read of earthquakes in Japan or ancient disasters.

Gloria's grip on his arm tightened; she urged him at least ten feet around a hairy vagrant who had been stumbling toward them.

"Aren't they *filthy*?" she whispered in horror. "You'd think they'd at least wash themselves. Soap's cheap enough. They ought to be kept off the avenue. They make it look so *depressing*!"

Hale thought of the flophouse with its one cake of caustic soap, its one faucet, and its five towels for sixty men.

She stared, fascinated, at the clumps of human wreckage. "Look, Billie-willie, we've passed dozens of places. Those things printed on the cards are jobs, aren't they?"

Hale nodded.

"Well," she pursued, "if they're *really* looking for work, why don't they go inside and get those jobs?"

Hale explained that they didn't have the advance commission. He knew that the jobless people walked along Sixth Avenue, stopping at signs, as he had, because it was better to have a hopeless hope than no hope at all.

Johnson would have enjoyed watching them; he regarded hope as one of his more satisfying torments. Hale didn't let himself think much about it. He had another idea in mind. "Let's not go down to the office today," he suggested.

She smiled brightly. "Oh, Billie-willie! Let's see the movie at the Capitol! All the girls were crazy about it—"

"Nope. We've seen enough movies. You don't mind, darling?"

"No, Billie-willie," she sighed fatalistically. "As long as—"

"—as long as we're together," he finished for her. He was pleased to note that he no longer minded so much knowing what she was going to say before she said it.

He took her into a cigar store and called his secretary at the office. "Miss Kay," he said, "look up Mr. and Mrs. Edgar Burke for me. They're the ones who inherited Nicholas Perry's estate, Superior, Wisconsin. We handled the case."

"Just a moment, Mr. Hale." He heard her walk away from the telephone, and listened interestedly to the clattering sounds of the office force.

He had often wondered whether they behaved so efficiently when neither he nor Johnson was there. They did; at least, he didn't hear the chattering of a normal staff. Johnson must have— "Mr. Hale? 333 Central Park West, sir. We have a complete record of their activities since they inherited the estate. Would you like me to read it to you?"

"No thanks. Central Park West, eh? Pretty high class. I won't be down to the office today, Miss Kay. If anything important turns up, leave word at my apartment."

He took a taxi uptown. Gloria wanted to know all about the Burkes; she hadn't known he had friends, and why hadn't he seen them until then? But Hale decided against telling her the spectacular story of his rise. She was a snob, as she couldn't very well help being. It would be better for her to meet the Burkes casually, without knowing their backgrounds.

The Burkes' apartment house was tall, modern, and impressive. "Pretty swanky," said Hale. "I think it'd be sort of nice living here next to the Park. When we look out, all we see is roof-tops."

"Oh, I wouldn't like it at all," Gloria replied, as if he had suggested a slum neighborhood. "Nobody worthwhile lives here, just climbers and rich criminals."

He shrugged and entered. The doorman followed. "Whom do you wish to see, sir?"

"Mr. and Mrs. Edgar Burke. My name is Hale, William Hale."

The doorman called the apartment on the house telephone and gave the message. He turned to Hale. "Would you mind speaking to him, sir?"

"Hello," said Hale cheerfully. "Mind if I come up?"

Delightedly he heard the wheezing adenoidal voice: "Which Hale are you? I can't place you, mister."

"Remember the sick guy in the rooming house—the one who wouldn't go to the hospital? That's me."

"Say! Sure, I remember you! Come on up. The apartment's 6K."

Entering the huge, ornate lobby, Hale gloated. The simple Burkes certainly ought to be happy, living here with an independent income. And he was responsible for the whole thing. It made him feel godlike to know that he could cause joy as well as misery.

He half expected the door of 6K to be open, with the

Burkes waiting for him. Instead it was closed. An eye stared coldly through the peephole. Then the door opened slightly, held with a chain, and a maid asked: "You folks selling anything? We ain't buying—"

"Not a thing." Hale grinned, though he didn't feel at all amused. "This is just a personal call." He was less certain of himself. Had wealth debased the Burkes? They never used to be suspicious.

You may think knitting needles are silent. Hale found they weren't.

Chapter XX

"YES, SIR," Burke said with dogged persistence. "Just like a dream, it was, wasn't it, Molly?" His wife nodded abstractedly.

"Just like a dream," he repeated. "This guy Perry kicking the bucket and leaving us his whole fortune. Molly...Mrs. Burke never even knew they were related, and here he cashes in—" Burke wagged his head. "You don't exactly look like you're starving, either. I wouldn't recognize you. You certainly looked mighty lou—bad, last time."

"I'm doing pretty well," Hale replied. There was an embarrassing silence. Hale took advantage of it to study the Burkes and their home. Something wasn't quite right. It certainly wasn't the apartment, which had obviously been furnished by a competent decorator.

The Burkes sat stiffly, smiling with a faintly despondent air, in graceful, slightly upholstered frame chairs placed with artistic precision on the sides of a false ivory-and-gilt fireplace.

"You have a beautiful place, Mrs. Burke," Hale said at last.

For a moment she brightened. "Isn't it nice?" Then she lapsed back into her fixed, uncomfortable smile.

Burke looked at the rug and closed his perpetually dry mouth to swallow. "I don't know. Either it's too nice for some, or it ain't nice enough for others. I mean...well, I hope you didn't get sore when Ada asked you if you were selling anything, did you?"

"Not at all," said Hale hastily.

Burke nodded gravely. "That's good. You know how it is. Some of your old friends come around to see how you're getting along. I mean they're all right. They're real friendly. Only—" He gestured feebly at the dainty room.

"They don't feel right," Hale supplied.

"That's it. They get kind of scared. Sit on the edge of their seats and get the hell out—sorry, Mrs. Hale—beat it first chance they get. Then there's the other kind—"

"Edgar!" Mrs. Burke protested.

"Well, I can't help it, Molly. They'll feel insulted if I don't tell them how come Ada asked them that. Folks we used to know, and strangers, too, trying to sell us all kinds of stuff. I don't know—"

"Don't listen to him," Mrs. Burke entreated. "He ain't used to having it nice. He keeps mooning around because he ain't...hasn't got so many useless friends."

Burke slapped his thighs and smiled bravely. "Cut it out, Molly! We're sounding like a couple of funerals. Sure, Mr. Hale, it ain't all fun, but we're having a real fine time for once in our lives. Ain't we, Molly?"

"You bet! Going to the Met—the opera, you know; plays—"

"Them I don't care for so much," Burke said thoughtfully. "I like a good picture myself; don't have to listen so hard and you can see faces. But then there's the summer. One good thing about dough—you don't have to sweat in the city, begging your pardon, Mrs. Hale. We can go to one of these summer resorts. Like Rockaway."

"Oh, you wouldn't want to go there!" Gloria said, speaking for the first time. "It's so cheap and dirty."

The Burkes looked uneasy. Burke said: "Well, maybe you're right. It's Newport we'll probably wind up in."

"Newport!" Gloria exclaimed. "Why, *nobody* goes there now!"

Mrs. Burke nodded wisely. "I told you so."

Burke stood up and glowered. "That's the whole damn trouble. When you got dough, you got to know where to go and have the right friends—"

"Edgar!"

He subsided, grinning shamefacedly. "Yeah, it's right you are, Molly. But it's kind of tough at first. Your old friends don't come around, and I can't say I blame them. I knew a fella, got himself a big job. Before that we used to be real bosom pals. Then I didn't feel so good, seeing him. He had plenty of dough to spend, and I had to be kind of careful.

That's how our old friends are now. The real ones, I mean. The others don't count. They're after what I feel like throwing them. And I ain't the throwing kind, so they stop showing up, too.

"The folks with our kind of dough"—he smiled resignedly—"we go around and say hello, and they don't return the visit. I guess they don't make friends as fast as poor folks, because they got to worry about who's out to trim them.

"But, hell, I'm having a swell time. I don't have to get up at five anymore to go to work. Soon as we get to know the ropes we'll get along swell. When I get to feeling kind of low, all I got to do is think about all the things we got to make us happy, and I perk up."

Mrs. Burke asked: "How about some coffee? Ada can bring it in a jiffy."

"No, thanks," said Hale, rising. "We have to be running along."

"How about coming around some night?" Burke offered.

"I'd like to," Hale evaded. "You know how it is. I'm pretty busy these days. I'll try to make it."

The Burkes looked hurt. "Thanks," said Burke, with unconvincing heartiness. "It was real nice of you to drop in." Significantly, he didn't mention seeing them again.

"You'll get straightened out soon," said Hale despairingly. "The first chance we get, we'll drop in again. It'll be soon."

Everybody shook hands and grinned frantically, and finally the Hales escaped and fled.

Hale was too depressed to speak. Gloria was silent for a while; then she said: "I know they're your friends, Billie-willie; but aren't they rather...common?"

"Don't call me Billie-willie!" he snapped. But it wasn't

merely irritation. His new self-confidence had been smashed. He remembered Sisyphus and his boulder.

Sitting in the office, trying to avoid the sight of Gloria, he thought as courageously as he dared. He got nowhere, because he couldn't bring himself to attack the fundamental issue. That he should cause suffering he expected, for that was Lucifer's partner's function. But that he could also cause happiness had been the counterweight to his unpleasant role. More than he knew, he had depended on the existence of that power.

He wondered uneasily why the Burkes weren't happy, despite his having given them everything to make them so. They tried to convince themselves that they were, but they were obviously miserable. From the fact that he tried to find arguments based on the premise that their unhappiness was either his fault or theirs, he should have guessed that the answer was buried deep in the roots of his basic philosophy. Digging it out would require tearing up the foundation of his character. What that would lead to, if he ever tried it, even Johnson's facile imagination might have had trouble foreseeing. The ruler of the Western Hemisphere would find his acceptance of the philosophy of Hell fatally shaken. When Lucifer's partner loses faith in the rationalization that permits him to cause suffering—hell literally breaks loose.

And there it was staring Hale in the face.

Chapter XXI

HALE DID GET some kick out of Johnson's next letter. Everybody likes to be appreciated, and the letter started off with a string of good, mouth-filling compliments on Hale's splendid success, the speed with which he was grasping the essentials of Johnson's methods, et cetera. The letter went on:

> Now that you have won your spurs, as one might say, in our somewhat unusual business, I have another task for you. You are no doubt familiar with the work of Fermi and Hahn in the

disintegration of the uranium atom. In the ordinary type of atomic disintegration, by which it has been possible to transmute elements for several years, the products are a new element of slightly lower atomic weight, and a few hydrogen and helium ions. The energy released, while large in terms of electron-volts, is much too small to keep the reaction going by itself; it is, therefore, necessary to continue to supply the target with a much greater amount of power from outside than can ever be gotten back in the form of atomic energy.

However, Fermi and Hahn discovered that uranium, under neutron bombardment, splits into barium, masurium, and several other elements such as iodine and caesium, with the release of enormous atomic energy of the order of 200,000,000 electron-volts. This discovery has aroused the hope that a self-sustaining, controllable atomic-disintegration reaction may be worked out at last.

I need hardly remind you of the effect of such a discovery on the technique of war. If the energy of ten pounds of uranium oxide could be released all at once, it could easily wipe a large city off the face of the globe. When the significance of these impending discoveries seeps down to the level of the average man in all countries, he will be made more apprehensive and unhappy than ever by the knowledge that, if a hostile government effects an atomic explosion anywhere in his neighborhood, he will have virtually no chance of escape. This will be much worse than the present threat of an air raid, which, while it can do great damage and kill thousands of people, cannot destroy more than a small fraction of a modern metropolis at one time, simply because of quantitative considerations.

As I say, the general impression among informed persons is that the discovery of such an atomic reaction is not far off. It is in fact nearer than they think. I have been observing the work of a Professor A. G. Dixon of Edinburgh, Scotland, and he appears to have the solution, though it has not yet been published, and will not be soon. I have had his figures checked by the most competent mathematicians of Europe, and they agree as to their correctness.

Professor Dixon has discovered that controllable atomic power cannot be obtained from uranium or any of its compounds—the reaction dies out too quickly to be self-sustaining. But it can be obtained from thorium, which is another heavy radioactive element.

In line with my policies, it is obviously undesirable that these facts become known immediately, as that would settle the question one way or the other. While it is still unsettled, we can keep the world's governments in a constant state of fear regarding the possible effects of atomic energy, and none of them will dare take any overt action in the absence of precise knowledge of the effects of this scientific advance.

We must, therefore, divert the attention of the world's physicists from thorium and keep it

concentrated on uranium, with which so many of them have been working since the Fermi-Hahn discovery. When they have finally discovered that they are up a blind alley, we can afford to let the truth become known.

I shall, therefore, take steps to prevent the publication of Dixon's work, and to divert this scientist from his present line of research. You will do what you can to renew the interest of American physicists in uranium. It has been flagging lately, since Columbia University's investment in a cubic foot of uranium oxide for research produced much interesting data but nothing tangible in the way of controlled, self-sustaining atomic power. To save you time, I might mention that the country's outstanding uranium enthusiast is Dr. L.R. Kammeyer, the head of the Physics Department at the Southwestern Institute of Technology.

This time Hale didn't sit around and mope. He knew next to nothing about atomic physics, but he plunged into the subject with as much energy as could be expected of a man of purely nontechnical background. In the course of his reading he learned a little about science and a good deal about scientists. Kammeyer was a dogmatic enthusiast; his institute was looking for a new endowment for a physics laboratory.

Hale reached into the Southwestern Tech envelope in the files and came up with a bunch of papers. One fell out and spun to the floor, as if inviting his attention. He picked it up; it was several sheets clipped together. Inside the blank cover page was a sheet of diagrams and four pages of small type, headed "United States Patent Office." Below this phrase, in bold-face type, he read:

**1,995,001
VACUUM TUBE**

**Willis N. Apostle, Los Angeles, Calif., assignor
to Southwestern Institute of Technology, Los
Angeles, Calif.
Application May 17, 1933, Serial No. 671,497
12 Claims (Cl. 41-126)**

Hale had never before seen a United States patent copy,
but the document proclaimed its nature clearly enough. He got
hold of Janos, the patent expert of Johnson and Hale's legal
staff. This worthy read the document through and whistled.

"Say," he said, "that's funny. This first claim dominates
every frequency-modulated radio receiving set on the market,
and I never heard of the patent before, though I know the art
pretty well. I don't *think* the Institute has been getting any roy-
alties from the radio manufacturers, though I can find out. If
they haven't, it probably means that this patent was taken out
back before people took frequency-modulation very seriously.
So the institute found no market for their rights, and forgot
about the thing. But now that all the broadcasters have
switched over to frequency modulation...jeepers, think of all
the infringements there have been in the last couple of years!
The patent only has a couple of more years to run, and we
can't sue for infringements that took place over six years ago,
on account of the statute of limitations. But we've still got the
radio manufacturers by the short hair, if we want to call the
Institute's attention to their position, and if that first claim isn't
anticipated by the prior art."

Hale frowned. "The radio companies are pretty tough customers, being hooked up with General Motors and people like that. Are you sure they couldn't string the litigation out indefinitely?"

"Not a chance. They can delay a little, of course, and that might be serious to somebody who didn't have the $10,000 that a normal infringement suit takes. But they can only stall for so long, and then we'll have them. Want me to go ahead with a preliminary investigation?"

"Yeah, sure, go ahead, Mr. Janos. Let me know."

"Oh, of course, Mr. Hale. You don't have to tell me that."

The first really hot evening, Gloria enjoyed lolling in a lawn chair on the terrace, and Eugene Banner relaxed completely. But Hale's tortured mind kept turning to the Burkes and why they weren't happy. After all, he asked himself, what did they have before? A monotonous routine: Up at five, sweep, scrub, shovel coal, make beds, argue rent out of people as poor as themselves, dispossess tenants with no place to go, make all the repairs in the house—all day and half the night, seven days a week, for just enough to keep them from going hungry.

Did they *like* that? Impossible! Then what was it? Well, no friends, discomfort in their elegant apartment; and you know how snobbish the well-to-do are: they haven't the easy friendliness of the poor, nor the self-confidence of the very rich, who can afford to make all kinds of friends.

Damn it, was that really the answer? If it was, how about all the people who make small fortunes? There were always plenty of them, rising from nothing. They managed to get by.

"Mighty nice up here," said Banner. "You can almost forget the trouble down below."

"What trouble?" asked Hale inattentively.

"Shaky market, factories closing, unemployment—"

"Oh, that," said Hale gloomily.

Banner sat up. "'Oh, that?' What the hell have you got to worry about that's bigger than the mess this country's in? Where do you come off, saying, 'Oh, that'?"

Hale didn't hear him. He thought: maybe it was his fault the Burkes were unhappy; the result of an error like that with his own spell. No, that couldn't be. He had told Johnson he had wanted the Burkes made happy, and Johnson had managed the whole thing.

Banner was shaking his arm. "What the devil's the matter with you, son? You're not the same shrewd, obstinate guy who busted into my office and said he wanted to marry my daughter. Come on, speak up!"

"I don't know what's the matter with him, daddy," Gloria complained. "Only this morning he was so full of life—"

"I'm all right," grumbled Hale. "Just some business worries." He thought, and went on cautiously: "When I got that partnership with Johnson, I bit off a little more than I expected."

It was partly true. The Southwestern Tech deal had gone off with the greatest of ease; the radio manufacturers had given in to the threat of an infringement suit without a struggle. The Institute now had enough money to keep its uranium research program going for years. But Hale found his enjoyment of this new triumph somewhat tepid. In an effort to take his mind off the Burkes, he had been thinking about his plan for keeping Bispham and his newspapers afloat. He had found the man to locate and rope his sucker: a Prince Igor Vershinin, who was a customers' man—female customers—for Titus, Farnsworth & Quinn, and who had assured Hale that nothing would be easier, for, of course, an appropriate consideration.

Banner resumed his seat. "That's it, is it? Can't say I blame you, with things the way they are. Say, you're usually pretty well posted. What do you think'll be the outcome?"

"Of what?"

"I mean, which way'll the country jump?"

"How should I know?"

"That's what everybody says. You know, Bill, it's enough to scare anyone out of reaching into his pocket. Isolation's all right—you can make real money at it, selling to both sides—but you got to depend on staying neutral. Get what I mean?"

"Yeah."

"Suppose you're an exporter. Until you know whom you can collect from, you're not going to sell to either side and take a chance of bad debts or embargoes. Or suppose you make automobiles. In case of war your plant'll be converted into an airplane factory, maybe. But if the country stays isolationist, you can go on making cars without changing all your equipment. Like this, though, you don't dare make either cars or airplanes, for fear of being stuck with a fortune in half-processed materials.

"Look here, Bill, I'm not a stubborn guy. I can see both sides. Either isolation or intervention would be a good thing, if we'd only decide on it." His voice rose to an agitated howl. "But for Pete's sake, let's make up our minds! This waiting around's what's putting capital in a panic, throwing people out of work, torturing the whole country!"

Hale squirmed uneasily. "Is it really making you so unhappy?"

"You bet it is! Advertising increases when sales drop. I haven't done so well since '32. But so help me, Bill, I'd cut my business to half of my lowest year if it'd mean getting rid of this...this suspense!"

Hale thought, Johnson would have assumed a mournful air of sympathy, but gloated inside. Why shouldn't he, Hale, gloat? But the knowledge of his success in making the hemisphere miserable merely depressed him and intensified his unreasonable sense of failure.

He stood up and clenched his fists for a moment. Then he sagged again. Whom was he defying? He was absolute ruler of half the world, accountable to nobody.

"Yeah, you're right," said Banner. "I'm tired, too. I'll run along and let you kids get to sleep."

Hale felt a warm, soft hand steal into his. He stood it as long as he could, then disengaged it as gently as his disgust would allow. Couldn't Gloria, the damned little fool, see his agitation?

Hale threw the newspapers on the floor, and punched the pillows behind him so he could sit up.

"Aren't you going to sleep, Billie-willie?" Gloria asked plaintively. He ignored her. Panic, fear, anxiety—why didn't the papers have the sense to shut up?

"Billie-willie, can't you do your thinking in the morning?"

"Please be quiet and go to sleep," he said tensely.

She blinked a tear out of her eye. "You don't love me any more!"

"I do." He heaved over on his side, with his back to her. This time he wasn't going to be wheedled out of thinking. Listening to her suppressed sobs couldn't possibly add to his unhappiness.

His unhappiness? He had tricked Lucifer into making him a partner for the express purpose of making himself happy.

He had appropriated everything he thought necessary to that end. Then why should he be wretched?

And why should the Burkes be unhappy with all the means of avoiding that state?

Was *anybody* happy? His father-in-law wasn't, despite his huge success in the advertising business. His new tool, Vershinin, wasn't, despite a good job with Hale's stockbrokers and the prospect of a fat commission when he had nailed Hale's picture-buying sucker. The Russian *emigre* was a likable enough chap, despite a broad streak of wooly mysticism. But his associates regarded him as a sort of glorified gigolo. Hale had guessed that Vershinin hotly resented this, but could do nothing about it; he could no more shed his accent and his manner than he could shed his skin.

If he could, with a little thought and guidance, make hundreds of millions unhappy, why couldn't he give happiness to a few?

The botching of the spell on himself and Gloria had been his fault. Had it? He hadn't known he was casting a spell until it was too late. Did that mean that Johnson had deliberately let him tangle himself in a degrading mess? Impossible! Johnson always lived up to his promises. *But had Johnson promised him happiness?* Hale thought back. He hadn't, actually; he had merely told Hale to get all the happiness possible.

But Johnson had understood the reason for giving the Burkes money. Why hadn't he warned Hale that they would be worse off than before?

Hale sat up. What was the last thing Johnson had said before he sailed? *"Anything you do, no matter what it is, will increase the misery and torments of the people, because that is how Hell is constructed!"*

Had Hale imagined that? He must have. There was no

logic in it. Even Lucifer must understand that to appreciate unhappiness you must have something to compare it with. To cause unhappiness, you ought to be able to create joy, or at least contentment. Certainly he could effect misery, but that wasn't the real test of a ruler. Could he create happiness, also?

Well, he could have made Gloria and himself happy, if he'd been told. He put that thought out of his mind, for it raised the suspicion of treachery. He refused to think about the Burkes. After all, he couldn't base his argument on the lives of four insignificant people.

The big thing was his paralyzing the hemisphere. He had done it, but he hadn't seen the magnitude of the results: Millions out of work; increase in the relief budget attacked by the economy lobby—and effectively, since they were now so powerful; hunger marches, riots, strikes, lockouts, freezing of credit— Out of all that torment and strife there should have been a little happiness. The isolationists and the economizers should have felt jubilant. But actually they were as frightened as the rest of the country.

If he and Johnson hadn't intervened, the government supporters, at least, would have been happy. Or would they? It seemed that people were unhappy no matter what you did. Then he *had* heard Johnson correctly? Like a sign shoved before his imprisoned eyes, a single point forced itself into his mind: the basic philosophy of Hell. The damned were in Hell because they deserved to be there, and if they belonged there their function was to suffer torment. But why didn't they know what their crimes were? And what *were* the crimes that deserved such frightful punishment?

He—Lucifer's partner—didn't know. But Johnson—Lucifer—would know. Lucifer would tell him.

Slowly, Hale straightened, realizing he had his arm drawn back to strike her—

Chapter XXII

GLORIA WAS TIRED of reading through the pile of magazines. They were only picture magazines, but at least they had more print on them than anything else she had looked at since they were married. Now she yawned and went back to her maddening knitting.

"Why don't you try to read something worthwhile?" asked Hale.

"I don't know. Those things don't interest me." She

shrugged, and went on with as much eagerness as if she were saying it for the first time: "I guess the only thing—"

"Yeah, the only thing you're interested in is us. Damn it, Gloria—" He hesitated.

"Are you angry with me, Billie-willie?"

"No." He wasn't. It was his fault that she would never outgrow adolescent archness, tearfulness, obsession with herself and him; not hers. It was his incompetence—or Johnson's treachery. He could no longer down that last suspicion. Until then he had been unwilling to call Johnson; it would be an admission of weakness.

Hell, he thought, always the damned intellectual; must find excuses, rationalizations for everything. If you want to call up, call up. What if Johnson's sore about the expense? Assert yourself! He picked up the telephone, said, "Get me Mr. Johnson," and put it down to wait.

When the instrument rang, Johnson's voice said: "Hello; that you, William?" Hale's sense of outrage went limp. It was odd how that friendly voice reassured him.

"Yes, this is Hale—"

"I'm very glad you called, William, though it isn't thrifty. Wouldn't a cablegram have done?"

"No!"

"Well, it saves the expense of a cable from this end. I was just about to send you one. Everything's finished here—signed, sealed, and delivered. Worked out splendidly, William. I really must congratulate myself. But now I'm leaving for Asia—"

"*Asia!*"

"Yes, my boy. Very imperative. The conflict there shows signs of faltering, perhaps stopping altogether. I must correct that. Hesitation now might lead to the collapse of the aggressor nation. How long it will take I have no idea. Perhaps a year, more or less."

Hale nerved himself for the plunge. "Look here: People are in Hell to suffer, aren't they?"

Johnson paused. "What's troubling you now, William?"

"A fundamental point. A damned fundamental one! Can people be happy or can't they? Or must everybody be unhappy, all the time?"

"Individually, a small amount of contentment, for a limited time, is possible. In the aggregate, man mostly suffers. Men may be happy for a while; mankind, never. Why?"

"Then they can't really be happy because they're being punished. Right?"

"Of course."

Hale gripped the telephone, hard. "Why are they being punished?"

Silence.

"What's the sense in it?" Hale pursued angrily. "Answer me!"

Slowly Johnson's voice asked: "You want to know their crimes?"

"Certainly. You don't slap a puppy without letting him know what he's done wrong. How can you punish human beings properly if they don't know that they're being punished, and why?"

"But, William, that wouldn't be efficient. If they knew where they were, they'd be resigned to punishment, and wouldn't suffer so much because they'd expect it. Then again, a lot of the weaker ones, instead of being activated by an instinct of self-preservation, would escape by killing themselves. The way the place is organized now, they suffer more in not knowing, since they torment themselves with futile hopes of happiness."

"All right. But why are they being punished?"

Silence again. Then: "I can't tell you that, William."

"You mean you won't!"

"No," the distant voice answered patiently, "I mean I can't. I'm abiding by our agreement faithfully, but the contract doesn't extend beyond this region. I can't tell you the secrets of the other domains; this is the only one I have power over."

Gloria was nudging his elbow, begging to be allowed to say hello to Mr. Johnson. Hale shoved her away.

"You tricked me, damn you! You said you've given me everything I needed for happiness!"

"I did. I fulfilled my promise."

"But you didn't tell me I could work spells. You didn't tell me how they worked, or how to go about it."

"Naturally, William. I let you learn the same way I did—by actual practice. It's much more effective than mere academic explanations. But I *did* warn you not to be hasty. I can't tell you to do this and not to do that. You wouldn't really have learned. You have to experiment to find out the dangers and limitations of your power."

"Damn you, don't be so glib! That doesn't go with me. You doublecrossed—"

A polite voice interrupted: "I'm sorry, sir; your three minutes are up. Do you want to go on talking?"

"Yes!" Hale shouted.

"No," Johnson's smooth voice answered. "Economy, William. Forget your peeve. It's childish. You can't escape first principles. Goodbye, my boy. I'll get in touch with you as soon as I'm settled." And the telephone went dead.

CHAPTER XXII

Hale furiously jiggled the studs on the phone to signal the operator. When the operator said, "Yes, sir?" he snarled: "Get me that number again!"

"I'm sorry, sir. Your party gave instructions not to be connected with your line. They say they won't answer."

Hale slammed down the receiver and glared at it. "You double-crossed me," he hissed. "You sat by like a grinning idol and let me make a horrible mess of my life! That was so I could learn by myself. You want me to punish people without telling them they're being punished or why. That's so the punishment'll be more subtle.

"Blast your fat hide, you white slug! I don't accept your first principles! I don't want any part of your philosophy of Hell! I'll undo everything you've done! I'll cause every bit of happiness I can! I'll show you I can create happiness!"

He caught the cowering Gloria in a kiss that made her murmur with pain and delight. That was the first step in his rebellion.

He yelled out the open window: "You have confidence! The winds will bring it to you! You can accomplish anything!"

Chapter XXIII

HALE'S FIRST CONCERN was to learn from his subjects how to fight their common enemy. With Gloria he visited the Stock Exchange, and was appalled by the hysterical defeatism of the traders. At a meeting between the administration and key figures in finance, industry, and labor, he and Gloria were inconspicuous observers. He had learned to use his connections to get himself into places where a mere clipping-bureau manager has no business being.

"It was enough to take the heart out of anyone," he told Banner afterward in New York. "A lot of cockeyed proposals came up, and a lot of sound ones, too—but everybody was scared stiff. All these big shots just sat around humming through their teeth. The whole thing's too big. Nobody really knows how to tackle it."

Banner rubbed his chin pensively. "Well, it *is* one hell of a big problem. Take the banks. They've got billions of dollars just lying around doing nothing; and let me tell you, it's a headache. You hear a lot about unemployed men, but unemployed capital is just as much of a problem. Why don't the banks extend credit? Well, industrialists don't want to draw too heavily on a future they're afraid of.

"And what are they afraid of? Taxes are high, though not as high as in a lot of countries. But there's the danger that they *might* become confiscatory. Reforms keep hamstringing expansion. The idea's supposed to be so business can't drive blindly into a boom that might get out of hand, like in '29. Everybody's scared of a boom, because it ends in collapse. I guess nobody's scared of the opposite—that maybe the whole system'll stall to a dead stop and just naturally fall apart.

If problems had only one side, Hale thought regretfully, reaching a conclusion would be so much simpler. Banner had given the orthodox financial explanation. That his analysis was entirely correct, from his point of view, only made the answer more elusive.

When Hale had, with much effort, succeeded in making Gloria dress poorly, he took her through the slums. The sight of families hanging onto food and shelter by the most precarious of holds infuriated him, but he could only grit his teeth, curse Johnson and himself, and divorce sentiment from reason until he could find the solution.

Defiantly but convincingly, a union official explained: "Sure, we stick with the administration. We'd be suckers if we didn't. Industry wants to expand, put in labor-saving inventions, cut down unit costs to meet competition. Sounds swell, doesn't it? But what happens to us?

"For a while we're sitting pretty, making all the stuff the machines can turn out, and without much work, either. Then what happens? We produce faster than the stuff can be sold. Goods pile up, and business gets slack, and we're laid off.

"Then when we've been on relief for a while, things pick up, which means the stocks are low enough to start work again producing more than we've got the money to buy, and the whole damned thing goes over the whole damned circle again.

"The administration wants to keep things going at a pretty even pace, so we don't produce too much or too little. And that suits us fine. Why not? Think we like to sit around waiting for inventories to drop so we can rush out goods and wait around again?"

"The way I see it," Hale said to Banner, "this hemi—this country was getting along pretty well until we had to make a decision on isolation or intervention. Then the government and the economy lobby fought each other to a standstill—"

Gloria had seated herself on his chair arm and was running her fingers through his hair. He tolerated the sensation until she whispered in his ear: "Billie-willie, can't you talk about something else? That's all I've been hearing for weeks, and it makes me dreadfully tired."

"Please, darling, this is very important."

Banner, ignoring the scene, declared: "Offhand, it looks like that might be the reason. I don't know, though. Wish I did."

"Why?" asked Hale.

"Well, take each one by itself. Those of us who are interventionists feel the country isn't strong enough to fight alone. We think we should jump on the aggressors before we're isolated and attacked. But those of us who are isolationists have the same idea, only the other way around. They don't want us to weaken ourselves by getting into a war that doesn't touch us at the moment. So they're for staying home and preparing until we can take on all comers."

While Banner filled a pipe, Hale pondered. Banner's reasoning seemed solid, so far.

"In other words," Hale said tentatively, "both sides are afraid."

Banner blew out a match. "Right! One side's afraid to let the enemy get too strong, and the other's really afraid to fight at all.

"I wasn't a kid when the last war started. We weren't anxious to get into it; but we felt that, once we did, the thing was as good as settled. Understand what I'm driving at? We had an idea we could take on the whole world single-handed. We don't feel that way now.

"Normally though—I mean when business is good—we'd all be isolationists. Not the cringing kind who mumble about putting our own back yard in shape. I mean a real stalwart kind of isolation, that says to aggressors: 'We're not going to pick on you, but just step over here and you'll get the hell knocked out of you'."

Hale thought he saw the answer; it was what everybody had been preaching, but from conflicting points of view. "You mean...?" he asked, to leave nothing unexplained.

Banner slapped his chair arm. "Confidence!" he roared. He went on to particularize, but Hale wasn't paying attention. He thought: Of course that was the answer. But what could he do about it? He could have remedied a purely material cause.

But the cause had nothing to do with lack of money, raw materials, labor, transportation, or management. It was purely psychological. And how do you go about remedying a psychological disturbance through an entire hemisphere? He explained his bewilderment to Banner.

"I guess you're right," Banner acknowledged. "It all depends on your angle, though. Taking a long view, you get that conception. But living in the present, seeing how things collapse when they get too good, and so on, sort of changes your idea. I don't know."

Hale jerked away from Gloria's exploratory hand and said vehemently: "But look here: if everybody felt the way we do—that this hemi—country has the most terrific future in the history of the world—we'd all feel confident, wouldn't we? And then we'd blast our way out of the depression by sheer confidence!"

"We certainly could!"

How, wondered Hale, do you give people confidence? By example? Well, if enough men expanded their business— Nonsense. The government had spent millions of dollars trying to revive trade, and had only made investors more fearful. Propaganda?

The silly optimism that the country's leaders had gone around radiating in the early part of the depression had been totally ineffectual. Laws? There were thousands of laws, periodically enforced and ignored, with no result but the creation of more fear and uncertainty.

Then the obvious thought struck him. He pushed Gloria's hand away and jumped up. He pointed a finger at his father-in-law. "*You* feel confident! Don't you?"

"I...I d-don't know—"

"You can't help feeling confident! Just look at what we've done and can do, and you'll—"

"Don't have to continue," said Banner, getting up and resolutely squaring his plump shoulders. "I guess I've felt that way all along, only I didn't have the guts to believe it." He slapped Hale's back. "I'm running along home. Got some plans for an expansion I've been carrying around in my head for years. All it needed was courage. Got plenty of that now...somehow!"

He marched away with his massive head erect, as if drums were beating. Hale fell back into his chair, his head in a whirl. In no time at all Banner had changed from a timid, depressed businessman to a confident, pugnacious, practically swashbuckling businessman. Hale couldn't get used to the prompt and drastic action of his spells.

He scarcely heard Gloria's: "Billie-willie, I've been a good girl, haven't I? I've listened to you and daddy talking about such awfully dull things, and I haven't even bothered you much. Can't I have the gang over tomorrow night for a party? A cute little party...just a tiny one."

Hale knew he had the cure, and it scared the wits out of him.

Chapter XXIV

HALE TOLD HIMSELF it was no time for intellectual hesitation. Act, man, act! Defeat Lucifer! Double-cross him as he tricked you! Revolt against the philosophy of Hell, disprove it, make man happy! But act!

Johnson loved paradoxes. That was one of the more horrifying aspects of Hell: ruthless confidence in the dictatorships, which were hopelessly poor and exhausted; nervous timidity in the democracies, which were drowning in wealth.

171

Unreasoning hope where there should be none. Those with nothing convincing themselves that they were miserable.

Fear lay beneath all this. Remove fear—no, that would be merely a negative cure. Instill confidence! Hale knew he could do it. Just to be sure, he watched Banner closely. With complete assurance, the advertising man had enlarged his business, and employed enough additional men to worry his Businessmen's Club members.

"I don't know what's come over him," Sam Furman, a shrewd chain-store clothier, had complained to Hale. "A pay-roll like this'll bankrupt him."

"Really? The country can stand plenty of expansion."

"Maybe," said Furman. "But I'll let the other guy experiment. I'm feeling my way."

"Just feeding, clothing, and housing everybody in this country would keep us busy. This is the richest nation in the world."

Furman nodded his somber head. "It all *sounds* good, but—"

"There aren't any buts," Hale snapped. "*You* have confidence. You've refused to face the facts, that's all."

The Businessmen's Club was astonished and cynically morbid when Furman bought a new factory, doubled the number of his employees, and opened stores in small towns. That was until Hale instilled confidence into them.

But after all, Hale thought, what did that amount to? A few indomitable businessmen bucking the inertia of the whole country; proof of his power; a goad to further effort. But he searched his mind furiously for means of casting the spell over the whole hemisphere.

One thing pleased him: he didn't have to use Johnson's sly, underhanded methods. His own were direct and humane.

CHAPTER XXIV

But was Hale a reformer? Not in the ordinary sense of the word. To prove he was capable of happiness, he had to prove he could make others happy, too. That meant reversing Hell's philosophy, and that, in turn, meant defeating Lucifer. The logic was inexorable.

But how? Key figures? He had thought so. But he couldn't reach all the large industrialists, bankers, labor leaders. And lack of confidence among the masses would sabotage and eventually stop any improvement resulting from an infusion of confidence into those on the tops of the pyramids. He had to make all his subjects feel equally confident. How? From his private office strings led to every section of the hemisphere. But he felt more helpless than ever, knowing that he had the cure but not the knowledge of how to use it.

He refused to allow the sound of Gloria's knitting needles to annoy him. But her incomprehension did bother him. Bother him? It drove him frantic. She yawned constantly, bored with everything she made no effort to understand, and irritated him by asking—at the most inconvenient times—to be amused. A life-and-death struggle against the first principles of Hell—and she knitted, placid, featherbrained!

He forced himself to drop that line of thought. It wasn't her fault, and she stayed with him loyally, almost without complaining. What more could he expect? Stick to the subject, Hale. How to spread confidence over the hemisphere— it should be easy—a mere psychological inversion for several hundred million people.

"Go ahead and do it," Johnson's professionally friendly voice said. The fat, commonplace face swam into his mind. The lunchtime chatter of the garment workers, in the street

173

below, merged into Johnson's taunting words. "Well, William? I see you are still hesitating. Why? After all, you are merely trying to contradict the basic philosophy of Hell, and upset all my plans. That should not be hard, should it?"

"Damn you!" said Hale aloud. "I know how it can be done!"

"Then why don't you do it? Shall I tell you why? *You don't know how!*"

"Oh, yes I do!" Hale shouted.

"Billie-willie!" A hand touched his arm. He jerked away, and yelled out the open window: "You have confidence! The winds will bring it to you. You can accomplish anything! You have the strength!"

"Billie-willie! What is it? You're not...going crazy, are you?"

He drew his hand across his eyes. "I started to crack, I suppose," he confessed. "I'm all right now. I won't let it get me." He wondered whether he was getting hallucinations. That wouldn't do: it would be playing into Johnson's hands.

"Let's take the day off, huh?" he said with forced cheerfulness.

"Oh, Billie-willie!" She caught his lapels and pulled his face down. "We can go to Mabel's tea! She wrote me and asked why we've been out of circulation for so long. *Everybody'll* be there!"

What the hell, he thought, what difference did it make where he went? The problem would be with him all the time. How to reach everybody in his hemisphere with the spell— rich and poor; humble and mighty; in cities, villages, and farms: asleep or awake; men, women, and children.

Actually, there was no longer any problem.

Chapter XXV

HALE MUST HAVE BEEN BLINDED by his hatred for
Lucifer, his revulsion at the philosophy of torment, and anxiety
over his own plans. Otherwise, being an observant man, he
would have noticed the change.

He was thinking: He could let the business run itself, and
devote all his time to making speeches. Of course, he couldn't
hope to address everybody, and he would have to learn Spanish
and Portuguese. But at least it was a half-way workable plan.

The telephone bell broke into his speculations. An excited voice cried into his ear, through an orchestration of yells: "Hello, Mr. Hale? Titus...Titus, Farnsworth & Quinn. What are you going to do about the market? Aren't you getting in on it?"

"I don't know," replied Hale absently. "What's going on?"

"*What's going on?* Holy smoke! Hear that shouting? Haven't you read the papers! Take a fast look at them and tell me what to do!"

Hale slid the newspaper on his desk around. It wasn't necessary to turn to the financial page:

BEARS IN HIBERNATION AS BULLS RUN MARKET TO SKY

During the first hour of a day that promises to set Stock Exchange records for trading, the entire list of shares jumped ten to fifteen points, with wild bidding and almost no selling, except from foreign investors, jamming the ticker until it was left hopelessly behind.

The Curb Exchange reports even greater gains and makes no secret of the fact that there is no limit to the prices stocks may eventually reach.

Informed sources highly influential in Wall Street refuse to credit statements from abroad that the situation is headed for unavoidable collapse because there had been, until now, no discernible corresponding gains in employment, national income, carloadings, production, foreign trade, or retail sales.

Chapter XXV

The consensus of investing opinion is that awakened confidence in the future of the nation...

...substantiating this claim, stock exchanges in all major cities throughout the Americas report gains as great as Wall Street's...

...in view of these facts, all reliable sources assert that a vast surge of public confidence has been responsible...

"Well, what'll it be?" demanded Titus. "Rails, utilities, heavy industry, mining, novelties?"

"I don't know—"

"Better get in fast, Mr. Hale! Everybody's buying and holding. While there's still foreign investors willing to sell—" He broke into a loud, harsh laugh, like the sound of a loaded cafeteria tray being dropped.

"They think we're riding for a fall! Why, damn them, there's no limit to what we can do! This is the biggest, richest, brainiest, nerviest damned country in the whole damned gutless world!

We'll show them a house for every family, a car in every garage, a chicken for every damned pot in every damned house, ten suits of clothing and fifty dresses for every man, woman, and child, hundred-million-dollar movies, hundred-billion-dollar industries, every man worth a fortune—"

"Hey! Wait a minute!" cried Hale. "What's the—"

"Not a thing, Mr. Hale. Nothing's wrong! Everybody's buying! What'll yours be? I've got a hot tip on a couple of million shares some damn fool foreign syndicate's holding. They're scared to hang on and scared to sell. I'll scare the pants off them and buy out for a measly couple of hundred million. You in on it?"

"I—"

"Of course, you are! We'll split it three ways; you, Johnson, and us!"

Hale yelled: "Where are you going to get a couple of hundred million?"

"From the banks, Mr. Hale. From the banks. They're practically giving money away. Sorry I can't go on talking; got to get started on this deal before prices double or triple. So long!"

Through the open window, Hale heard for the first time the street clamor of laughing voices; voices not dull and defeated as before, but somehow buoyant, eager—*confident*.

It didn't take Hale long to find the answer. Of course, it seemed absurd, the idea of casting a spell on the whole hemisphere by shouting through an open window. But he couldn't very well ignore the evidence.

He snatched Gloria's knitting away and dragged her up. "Come on!" he snapped. "We're going out."

"Can y' imagine the guy's noive? A lousy hundred a week! I says, 'Zimmerman,' I says, 'you don't want a cutter,' I says, 'you want a butcher.' He says, 'Louie, I kept you when things was slow,' he says. I says, 'Zimmerman things has changed. I'm going in business for myself,' I says—"

"Hunnid a week! I laughs at my boss when he offas me a hunnid and a quawta. I sure tol' him wheh to put his lousy job. Me—I'm gonna cawna cloaks and suits, see if I don't!"

"*Haw! Haw! You?* How you gonna buck *me*?"

A short, puffing, harried man waddled toward the knot of boastful gabblers, crying plaintively: "Boys! Boys! I'm renting a whole flaw, maybe the whole building yet, but woikas I got to have. Name ya prices! I'll meet any offer in the city!"

"You can't pay what we're asking—"

The businessman wrung his hands in agony. "I don't care *what* you're asking! Woikas I got to have! I'm telling you, I'm going to be the biggest clothing manufacturer in the *woild!* Only, woikas I got to have!"

"Listen to him!" said a meek-looking runt sarcastically. "*He's* gonna be the biggest manufacturer! What about me? Soon's I get down to the bank and borrow a few hundred thousand, I'll buy him out. I'll buy out everybody in the block; then I'll start working on the rest of the city."

Hale didn't know whether to follow the unhappily confident employer or the derisively confident employees. Watching either of them solve their problems would be interesting. Still—hallucinations? He was pretty sure he was sane; but sometimes under great strain minds crack. He asked Gloria: "Did you hear what I heard?"

"What is it, a strike? Everybody's walking out of the buildings."

"Did you hear them refuse a hundred and a quarter a week?" he insisted.

"Yes. Then it's a strike, isn't it?"

Hale knew he hadn't imagined the crowds pouring into the streets, with screaming employers chasing after them. But a strike? If this was happening all over his hemisphere, it was the biggest, most universal walkout in history! And not a simple walkout either, but a unanimous desire to become employers!

Hale was satisfied to follow along with the crowd. Gloria clung to his arm and shrank against him for protection from the jabbering throng who, she probably thought, weren't quite clean. He listened.

"Sure I come to work this morning, same as always. I see

this ad in the paper—"

"The bank ad? Yeah, I saw it, too. So what'd you do?"

"I go in and show the boss this ad and he says he'll give me a raise if I don't quit and then the rest of the gang pile in with the same story about quitting and—"

It was a repetition of the stories being told all around him. Hale drew Gloria over to a newsstand that was being closed. Every newspaper had been sold, but for half a dollar the agent offered him a soiled, torn copy of the *Socialist Appeal*. He got behind the stand and looked through the paper. The first of six full-page advertisements cried out:

THE BANKERS' TRUST COMPANY BELIEVES:

1) In the future of America! No other single country in the world possesses the lavish resources that lie under our feet and everywhere around us, begging to be developed.

2) In the ability of Americans! Single-handed, starting with nothing whatever, our ancestors raised America from a wilderness to the greatest industrial power on earth!

3) In ourselves! We have aided, with money and sound advice, in the birth and expansion of a staggering number of American industries, the names and histories of which strike pride in the heart of every true patriotic American!

WE GLADLY ASSUME THE RESPONSI-BILITY:

Of assisting to full growth the most amazing national rebirth in the history of humanity! We are, therefore, prepared to extend every aid: financial, managerial if necessary, advisory under all circumstances, since we base our advice on the experience of ninety-seven years of successful finance:

TO EVERY MAN WHO CAN SHOW PROOF, FINANCIAL OR OTHERWISE, THAT HE HAS A SOUND, WORKABLE, CONCRETE BUSINESS IDEA AND LACKS ONLY SUFFI-CIENT FUNDS FOR ITS PROPER DEVELOP-MENT OR EXPANSION!

In order to remove all obstacles in the path of national confidence in our great and glorious future, the Bankers' Trust Company:

REDUCES INTEREST TO 1/2 OF 1%! NO COLLATERAL! NO CO-SIGNERS! ONLY A ROUTINE CHECKUP OF YOUR PLAN! WE BELIEVE IN THE FUTURE OF THIS COUN-TRY!

Hale pursed his dried lips and tried to whistle in amazement. The *Socialist Appeal* taking a bank's advertisement! A quick glance at the other bank's ads in the paper had shown him only a remarkable similarity to the Bankers' Trust effusion. But on the next page, in big block letters, he found:

WORKERS! THE *SOCIALIST APPEAL*, ON BEHALF OF THE PARTY IT REPRESENTS, STRESSES THE IMPORTANCE OF TAKING FULL ADVANTAGE OF THE BANKS' OFFERS! BY DEVELOPING THE RESOURCES AND MEANS OF PRODUCTION OF OUR COUNTRY YOU WILL BE ABLE TO INHERIT THE RICHEST FRUITS OF CAPITALISTIC CIVILIZATION! THE GREATER OUR INDUSTRIES, THE GREATER OUR EVENTUAL PROSPERITY! IF WE ARE TO SEIZE POWER, LET US BE SURE THAT CAPITALIST EFFICIENCY AND ORGANIZATION HAVE CREATED THE WORLD'S RICHEST COUNTRY FOR US! WORKERS OF AMERICA, WE ARE CONFIDENT OF THE FUTURE THAT WILL MAKE US MASTERS OF OUR FATE!

Hale put the paper in a trashbasket and drew Gloria back in the crowd. They were on Seventh Avenue, moving uptown through halted, honking traffic and cops, afoot and on horseback, who seemed more anxious to join them than to keep them orderly—swarms of men and women, boys and girls, streaming out of side streets and buildings to join the river of people, yet somehow not losing their identities. Mobs are generally homogenous in mood and object.

This mob outwardly resembled others; its aim was one spot; its one emotion was cheerfully belligerent self-confidence.

But each atom of the mass had a strictly individualistic goal.

At Fortieth Street they jammed to a stop, and stood packed and clamored good-naturedly at the top of their lungs.

"Let's get away from this," Gloria begged in a small, timid voice.

But Hale was fascinated. He balanced on his toes and peered over head. On the outer fringe of the crowd a sound truck managed to get fairly close to a bank building on the east side of the avenue. By pressure from the front, Hale knew that people were forming a path for it. Presently he saw the truck door swing open with difficulty. The loud-speakers crackled and burst into a roar:

"Friends, the directors of the City Bank take this opportunity to thank you for this splendid response to their offer. We must admit frankly, however, that your response has swamped us.

"We must ask your co-operation in giving us time to analyze the situation and modernize our credit apparatus. In this request we are not alone. Every bank and credit organization in the Western Hemisphere"—Hale began trembling with anticipation—"has been unable to meet the demands put upon it.

"Therefore a new, highly efficient Pan-American credit organization, embracing every bank, investment house, trust fund, loan society, in either of the American continents, all co-ordinated to the last degree, is swiftly being put into operation.

"You can readily see, my friends, that the financiers of America—of Greater, More Prosperous America, the America of both continents—believe implicitly in the magnificent future of our half of the world!"

The crowd cheered. Hale felt thrilled, and listening to the suave voice calmed Gloria, though she still vainly tried to avoid bodily contact.

"There are certain limitations we have temporarily agreed to impose," the speaker roared on. "While we are unconditionally prepared to finance any and all sound, practical business ideas, we must insist on a certain amount of capital on the part of the borrower—"

The mob began to mutter resentfully.

"In that decision," the speaker added hastily, "we do not show lack of confidence. The amount is arbitrary...nothing at all if the idea shows exceptional promise. But in most cases we must ask equal confidence on the part of the borrower, in that he should demonstrate his business ability by acquiring a certain amount of his own capital.

"With wages skyrocketing"—the voice became humorously deprecating—"that should prove no major obstacle to any really industrious, self-confident worker, should it?"

The crowd laughed, cheerfully cocksure.

"In return for your co-operation, the Pan-American Credit Corporation and all its constituent units will extend unlimited credit—in accordance with its very simple conditions, which will be determined very shortly—unlimited credit, I repeat...with not the slightest charge for interest! All we ask is the opportunity of purchasing shares in the companies we finance!"

The crowd screamed approval. Hale searched his mind for a trick.

"Now please return to work and concentrate on saving capital!"

The mob broke up leaving Hale wondering. He caught the sleeve of a well-dressed, professional-looking man.

Hale guessed him to be a lawyer. He asked: "Do you think that's on the level...no interest on loans?"

"Certainly," replied the stranger with disdain. "Why shouldn't it be on the level?"

"Well, I don't know. How will the banks make money?"

"Evidently you don't understand economics. With the enormous potential earning capacity of this country, merely taking shares will bring in far more than the old obsolete method of asking repayment of loans plus a fixed rate of interest. In companies with exceptionally bright futures, the banks ask the opportunity of buying additional shares."

"Oh," Hale breathed and turned to find a taxi willing to sell him a ride. He thought, if he'd gone to the bank the day before, and offered merely an idea and the option of buying stock in a non-existent company, in return for a loan—well, who was loony now?

Hale and Gloria stood on the rim of a huge excavated lot. In his absorption in what was going on there, Hale ignored his discomfort. But Gloria wailed: "Oh, Billie-willie, it's so *hot*! Why can't we go swimming?"

"Later, darling," he said abstractedly.

"But you always say the same thing. You don't have any consideration for me anymore. You don't love me!"

"Oh, hell," he said irritably, and gave her a sweaty kiss.

When he turned back, a quarrel was starting in the center of the half-completed foundations. Hale wavered; he couldn't leave Gloria, nor could he heartlessly ask her to climb down the dusty embankment.

He waited impatiently until it was over. Then he called the contractor, who came over, angry and red. "What's the trouble, Reading?" he asked.

The contractor stopped smearing his handkerchief across his forehead. "Trouble?" he shouted. "It is and it ain't. A year ago I'd have fired every damned one of 'em, only now I can't replace them."

"What do you mean—it is and it ain't?"

"I mean trouble. I guess I'm getting used to it, so it ain't really trouble. See those guys down there?" He pointed.

"Of course. What about them?"

"I'm the contractor on this damn job. That's supposed to mean I get contracts, buy materials, get blueprints, and hire all the men. Ain't that so? Well, it ain't...not anymore!"

Hale murmured uncomprehending sympathy.

"Don't feel sorry for me," Reading bristled. "I can lick them. They're only the guys who lay the foundations. After them come the steel workers and the carpenters, bricklayers, plumbers, electricians, plasterers, and so on. Well, they make me divide up the contract so each man's working for himself. You know, like a...uh—"

"Co-operative?"

"Yeah." Reading flapped his soaked handkerchief and stuffed it in his pocket. "Every man for himself. They made me tell how much dough there was in the contract, and then they figured out what everybody should get. Damn it, I tell you they're a bunch of communists!"

Reading spun around in the grip of a heavy, cement-whitened hand. "None o' that, mister!" a cement porter threatened. "Everybody on the job figures out what it costs him to work. All we want is a profit over our expenses. We're in business, same as you."

Reading snarled: "Yeah; but you're asking a hell of a big cut!"

"You bet!" the worker grinned and ambled away with

his wheelbarrow. "There's plenty o' dough for everybody, and more coming!"

The contractor glowered. "See what I mean? They pay me a commission for getting the contract and buying materials. But *I* got the whip hand, bud! I'm the guy who has the blueprints and contracts! Just let them keep on getting funny—"

Tactfully, Hale didn't mention the possibility of their refusing to work. Reading would have been as confident as before of his ability to break his workers—"his" no longer. And the workers would have been confident, even had they known of his threat to refuse access to the blueprints, that they could get along splendidly without him.

It was all very confusing. Hale had never thought that some day workers might hire their bosses, which was what it amounted to. Who could have imagined that banks would be distributing money almost without asking questions?

Unlimited credit for unlimited expansion! He stopped there. His mind, battered by so many previous improbabilities, refused to go as far as the question: they'll all get capital; and then?

"Isn't it cute, Billie-willie?" cried Gloria.

Chapter XXVI

BY THE MIDDLE OF AUTUMN, Hale was no longer fearful. Like the rest of his hemisphere he had lost the capacity for astonishment. Generic man can adjust himself to almost any environment, and Hale adjusted himself to the change— a little late perhaps, because he was one of the two people in the western world who hadn't been affected.

Outwardly these new processes appeared very complex. They were certainly hectic and swift. But they could be reduced to one word: Co-operation. For instance, a price was set on the construction of the factory; the workers broke that price down into units: so much for each man in each branch of construction. The manufacture and installation of the machinery, the operation of the factory, and the selling of the product were similarly organized. The result was that every man was his own employer. That incidentally removed the possibility of individual expansion, because nobody would work for fixed wages.

Hale had experienced the same difficulty as other employers with his servants and his and Johnson's office force; he had had to let some of the former go, and kept the remainder only by paying astronomical wages; the latter were finally satisfied with a contractual arrangement that he assured them was a form of profit-sharing.

On the whole, though, general expansion of an entire co-operative was limitless. That raised the individual profit along with the whole, and also did away with anarchic competition, in which everybody strove to be kingpin of his particular industry.

Realization of that made Hale smile grimly. What could have defeated Johnson more completely? The devil loved class, civil, and international war; but he never ignored the possibility of dog-eat-dog competition, with everybody fighting everybody else for existence. Let him come over here now, and see how far he'd get!

But eventually gloating over a vanquished enemy, even one of Lucifer's stature, loses its edge. Hale had to go on from there. Unlike stories, a man's life seldom stops short at the climax; he lives past it. What should he do next? He was resolved not to make a diabolical plan, like Johnson's. Neither was he going to reverse his destination. For in the abstract, like most men where the future of mankind was concerned, Hale had always been something of an idealist. Like most men, also, his idealism and his self-seeking were two water-tight compartments in his mind. But now, having seen his subjects work together in harmony for their common benefit, Hale had become—the truth must be faced—a reformer, with himself as Leader, of course.

His hemisphere ran smoothly enough; when one of the rare major problems came up, the self-confidence of his subjects always found a solution. The only source of danger that Hale foresaw was Johnson. What Johnson could do to undermine his Utopia, Hale couldn't imagine, but he didn't underestimate his enemy's cunning. But Johnson seemed lost somewhere in Asia. Now and then Hale got a cablegram from him. They were terse, cheery messages, giving little information and asking for none, mostly because, he said, he didn't know where he would be next.

By the first snowfall of winter Hale had become contemptuous. The change was too firmly established for Johnson to wreck it. So Hale turned to whatever problems might still disturb his hemisphere. What was there to do? Finance? Nothing so complicated could have run with less friction. The Stock Exchanges? Nobody sold. A few minutes after new shares were issued they had all been snapped up, and there was nothing more to buy. Politics? In prosperity it rides at the tail of the procession, keeping its hands ostentatiously in its own pockets for fear of rocking the boat. Unemployment? Class warfare? National income? They had all ceased to be problems.

Sitting in his office and reading reports, Hale wore a perpetual grin of victory, even when Gloria knitted or nagged to be amused. She was just a minor annoyance. He still loved her—that couldn't be altered—but her beautiful, omnipresent face, with its pout of boredom and its other expression of coy affection, had lost a lot of its appeal. Love, he realized wistfully, should be renewed by judicious absences, and that, of course, was impossible for them.

But what the hell! Ore and steel production were at 100% of capacity, even though mines and plants would shortly be double those of a year ago. Automobile production was 240% above the previous peak. Airplane production, a mere beginning in serial manufacture, was 5,000 a week, and could be quadrupled if trained personnel kept pace. Carloadings were 73% higher than in 1929. Retail sales: *1,242% above the same month of the year before!*

If Hale hadn't taken Gloria through the stores, he could never have concretely realized how many people were purchasing wildly, buying goods almost before they were unpacked; how many new stores there were. Of course, since the Hales were merely observers, their own behavior in buying only what they needed seemed entirely normal to them.

Now Hale began to play with the notion of invading the rest of Lucifer's territory, and turning the Eastern Hemisphere into another Utopia. He'd make his double cross really complete! Of course, he'd have to wait for the dictatorships to collapse. If he tried to hurry the process they would try to pull the rest of the world down with them. Hale wasn't motivated by humanitarian pacifism, since a war couldn't be a personal danger to him, and since he would live to see all the millions of people who would have become casualties die of other causes in any event. But he hated the thought of giving Johnson the gratification of another war. The dictatorships looked extremely shaky, and it wouldn't be long. Hale rubbed his mental hands together in anticipation.

Chapter XXVII

THE HALES HAD A DATE with Banner at the Cordova. That put Hale in something of a fix. He disliked driving himself in heavy traffic. His chauffeur, since the change, had developed a driving technique alarmingly like the flight of a swooping swallow, in perfect confidence that he could avoid all obstacles by the necessary thickness of a razor blade. Hale couldn't reprimand the man, for fear he would carry out his oft-repeated threat to quit and go in business for himself.

Even the immutable Hamilton had lost an astonishing amount of his normal servility. "Y' see, Mr. Hale, I'm staying on because I think you're a jolly good bloke to work for. I like you. But if I change my mind, it'll be cheerio and goodbye to you!"

Hale could hardly drag Gloria through the subways in an evening dress. So he put up with the chauffeur's tactics, pressing the floor with his foot at every intersection. At Sixth Avenue they were held up by fire engines.

The familiar bells and sirens had been egregiously frequent lately, thought Hale.

It hadn't occurred to him before that confidence with many people might result in their being careless with matches. It was a possibility; he'd have the office force get him up a report.

Just before they got to Longacre Square, the car stopped suddenly. There was a commotion up forward, and a spatter of shots, quite loud over the low roar of the theater district.

Something hit Hale in the face; just a touch. It was a fragment of glass, not much bigger than a sand grain. There were three neat holes in the side window of the limousine, with spiderwebs of cracks around them.

Past the chauffeur's head, Hale caught a brief glimpse of a man lying in the sidewalk. Then his view was cut off by swarms of civilians and cops.

The chauffeur talked to one cop who stood beside the car for a moment; then turned to the Hales. "Guy tries to hold up a jewelry store, all by himself, right under the nose of a flock of cops. Must have been overconfident, I guess.

They got him, and a couple of folks got hit by strays. I don't know if they were—gee!" His eye fell on the three holes. "We almost got some ourselves!"

CHAPTER XXVII

Hale didn't see the sense in explaining that he and Gloria had been perfectly safe, no matter how much lead was flying around. It wouldn't have made the chauffeur happy to know that *he* was still vulnerable.

That was a concrete example of a tendency that had appeared in a report submitted to Hale two days previously at the office. There were fewer criminals, but more crime.

Those who had robbed to keep alive had reformed, since it was so easy to make an honest living now. But those who robbed for the fun of it, who preferred one crooked dollar to two honest ones, were more active than ever, being full of confidence in their felonious plans.

It was remarkable that Hale and Banner could talk at all in that noise. Stripped showgirls and dancers and strident comedians kept leaving the stage, to perform in the newer, more obtrusive manner among the customers' tables. Gloria had her chair turned away from Hale and her father and watched delightedly.

Banner passed a sheaf of papers back to Hale. "So what?" he grinned.

"Well, I just wanted to get your opinion," replied Hale evasively. "The graphs for last month show production at an increase, and sales are falling off pretty heavily...enough to make you take notice, I think."

"Scared?"

"N-no." Hale smiled back, a trifle weakly. "I just wanted to find out what your opinion was. And you'll admit it's a pretty serious business when all the insurance companies go *pfft*."

"Oh, them. Nothing to worry about. Sure, the accident rates are up, and people aren't taking out policies anymore.

But the liquidation of the companies won't even make a ripple in our prosperity. I know one insurance man who says he's glad to get out of the business. Says what he's always wanted to do is cartooning, and he's perfectly confident he can make a go of it."

Banner had to stop while a group of girls, ostensibly goaded on by a ringmaster with a beribboned whip, surrounded him and kissed his leonine face. Gloria and the crowd got an immense kick out of the performance. When the performers had left, Banner scrubbed the lipstick off his face.

"My opinion?" he asked, still red and laughing. "This is a hell of a place to talk business. Well"—he drew his chair closer to Hale so he wouldn't have to shout—"naturally I spoke about the rise in inventories with a few of my biggest accounts. They feel the same as me—nothing to worry about."

"But look," Hale said earnestly, "if sales keep going down and production keeps rising—"

Banner patted his son-in-law's arm. "You're hopping yourself up for nothing. What of it? Got to expect it. At first the people were starved for everything, and when they got the dough they bought everything in sight. Like a refugee from one of the poorer dictatorships. Ever see one? They can't get any kind of fat there.

"When they come here that's about all they eat—butter an inch thick and fat with or without meat. But when that particular hunger's satisfied, they quit. Same with our people. When they get about two of everything they need, they naturally stop buying so fast."

A fight had broken out among the customers; a small, slight man, who might, before the change, have been expected to have better sense, was wading into a two-hundred-pounder, swinging wildly. When a couple of waiters had carried off what was left of the little man, and the noise had subsided below boiler-factory level, Hale went on with his questions. "But what'll we do to get rid of our surplus if that's the case?"

"Sell, my boy! We'll sell!"

"But to whom?"

"That's the easiest part. The dictatorships have cut adrift from the economic world, with their principle of self-sufficiency. Won't work out, of course. All it really means is starving so you can pay for guns. Sooner or later news of how well off we are will leak into those countries, and they'll throw out the big shots and stop their self-sufficiency policy. We step in and sell 'em stuff!"

"Oh," said Hale. "Sure."

They sat in silence for a while. Hale stared indifferently past Gloria's lovely profile at the boisterous floor show. The crowd was clamorous and thirsty, and insisted on being part of the entertainment. Male and female drunks staggered out on the floor in imitation of the performers; the rest contented themselves with snatching entertainers to their tables and making them drink.

Visiting Europeans claimed to find a resemblance between decadent Roman carnivals and the pursuit of amusement in Hale's hemisphere. Hale was shrewd enough to see the difference.

The effete Romans accepted entertainment passively.

The Americans amused themselves. They drank whatever liquor was nearest to pure alcohol, usually out of the bottle; they danced the rowdiest dances imaginable; they stumbled onto the floor or stage and took over from the professionals.

Merely watching tableaux of girls, no matter how naked, would have required too much disinterested contemplation, and Hale's hemisphere was anything but disinterested or contemplative. It demanded action, with itself as the most active participant. Its search for amusement, Hale had to admit to himself, was somewhat desperate.

"Nope," said Banner thoughtfully, "it isn't getting rid of our surplus that's worrying me."

"Isn't it?"

"No. Get this straight! I've got just as much self-confidence as the next guy! I know we've got a future no other country in history can match. Only"—he glared at the writhing mass of audience and performers— "a guy my age can't help stopping and thinking now and then. Look at them! They're what I'm worrying about, the half-witted nippleheads!"

"You're worried about *them?* How come?"

Banner filled a pipe with unnecessary care, as if daring the management to interfere. "They're not happy. Got more than they ever dreamed of and still they're not. Miserable, in fact—"

"They're—" Hale began trembling. He whispered: "What makes you say that?"

"Well, they are, only they don't know it. They're trying to convince themselves they're having a swell time. Only they're not. Here's how I look at it, Bill—everything came too easily. I was brought up having whatever I liked; always lived that way.

These poor devils never had anything. Now all they want is practically theirs for the asking. They can buy anything they want. But, hell, you can't keep buying like a maniac all your life. That hunger gets satisfied, same as any other."

Hale laughed derisively. "Anything they want is theirs...so they're unhappy! You're crazy!"

"Maybe," Banner said obstinately. They paused while a drunk shuffled over and asked Gloria to dance. Hale knew why she clutched with horrified desperation at his hand. But Banner looked sentimental and mumbled something about their having been married nearly a year and still—

"Take yourself as an example," he said when the drunk had wandered off. "Remember when I offered you a job at ten thousand a year with hardly any work connected with it? How many guys would have thrown away a chance like that? At that time, I mean. But what did you do?"

"I had other plans," said Hale, wishing that Gloria would release his hand.

"Sure. Bigger plans. A damn big fortune. A twenty-nine-room apartment. Five cars—so you walk most of the time. Summer home you didn't step into all summer. Shooting lodge, and you never shoot anything—"

Hale sat still, knowing that if he took out a cigarette his hands would shake. "What are you getting at?"

"That yacht of yours. Say, even now, how many people can afford a yacht? But when did you go on a cruise last? A couple of times after you first got it, and then you lost interest. Same with these poor suckers. It isn't getting what you want that gives you the kick, especially if you get it easily."

"No?"

"Course not! It's the anticipation! Why, the day you crashed my office...you certainly looked lousy, but underneath those rags and whiskers you were just about the happiest, most *vital* guy I'd seen in years! That's because you were anticipating—"

It was true; Hale could look back and see that.

"And ever since then you've been sort of lifeless.

199

Understand what I mean? You just sit back now. You're about the unhappiest guy in the world. You don't give a damn about what you own. Take it for granted—"

Hale had to be honest with himself; he did derive no pleasure from his material possessions. But that was because of Johnson's trickery. The victorious struggle against Lucifer and the philosophy of Hell gave him enough satisfaction to compensate for everything else.

"Why, hell, Bill...Gloria's practically your whole life. Being with her's about the only fun you get!"

Hale tried not to wince visibly. His only pleasure! Lord! He had to love her, but his spell didn't blind him, which was unfortunate. If it had, he might not have been so disgusted as he watched the delight that she got out of brawls like this one.

"I'll tell you, Bill, my idea is that getting over the buying craze is a healthy thing."

"Yeah? Why?" asked Hale, his voice almost normal again.

"Well, here's my analysis. What happens when all of a sudden you can get anything you want? You buy like mad, naturally. But you get over it. I think all this excitement and...well, call it subconscious misery are just transition. See what I mean?

"These folks will adjust themselves to prosperity. They'll develop a sense of proportion, when they see that a new hat or shoes or a bigger house isn't the main thing in life. Then they'll settle down and think of really important matters.

"They think they can stop at success, but they can't. Success looks big to anybody who hasn't got it; he thinks he can ride along the rest of his life enjoying it. He can't. He has to get another goal."

CHAPTER XXVII

Hale had already discovered that phenomenon. He knew that after even such a huge victory as defeating Lucifer, he'd have to find another mountain to roll his boulder up. He'd do it, too. He'd invade the other half of Hell and snatch it from Lucifer.

"There was an aim vast enough for anyone: all Hell a Utopia! But even after that he wouldn't rest. There would always be more goals to anticipate.

"So I guess I'm not really worried about them, after all," said Banner. "The dictatorships are about ready to cave in. You notice they're still beating their chests and roaring, but they aren't making any more concrete demands.

"There's a real sign of weakness for you! We'll pile up a little surplus, but when the dictatorships fall we'll have all we can do supplying those poor devils."

He nodded complacently and shoved his chair back. "Go ahead and give the little woman a whirl, son. That sounds like a nice dance number."

Hale got up and opened his arms to Gloria. Her shiver of joy touched him. Her yielding body and generous affection were, for the moment, ends in themselves.

Even Banner, for whose shrewd intelligence Hale had great respect, found Hale's hemisphere nearly perfect. The period of adjustment would soon be over; the surplus would find markets. Lucifer would finally be dethroned. What more could he ask?

That same week Hale got a telegram from Johnson, saying that he would return on the 26th, and would Hale please meet him at the airport.

The 26th — The date had some obscure significance for Hale. Was it the anniversary of his partnership? Probably

201

something like that. It made no difference. All that counted was his own anticipation.

Johnson's wire had sounded cheerful enough, or at least had not been abusive. But Hale was willing to bet that Lucifer's repulsively fat face wouldn't be quite so jovial. *That* was anticipation—meeting the vanquished all-powerful!

Chapter XXVIII

HALE STAGED IT WELL. He and Gloria stood in solemn dignity at the edge of the enormous field. Walking across any field makes any figure seem crawling and insignificant. Therefore, he would let Johnson march, small and lonely, toward him over the airport.

If he had had complete control over such matters, he would not have taken Gloria along. She squirmed and craned her neck, anxious to see Johnson, which somewhat spoiled the effect. Nor would he have made it so bitingly cold. Much as he wanted to remain haughtily motionless, in somber majesty, he had to flap his arms and stamp his feet now and then. That reminded him that he would have to do something about the weather.

Johnson was probably responsible for the condition that "Man is born to shiver and perspire," with, of course, just enough enjoyable weather to make the extremes more uncomfortable.

Alexander P. Johnson came out of the airliner and climbed heavily down the portable steps. Hale's heart pumped swiftly. At that distance there seemed to be no change. It was too far, Hale reasoned. Watch for the sagging shoulders, the plodding walk.

But, round head erect, belly heaving up and down at every step, Johnson marched toward him without a trace of self-consciousness, the soles of his shoes jerking up into clear view at every step.

Hale had to admit that he appeared as confident as ever. When Johnson waved his short arm, Hale quivered. But he shrugged off his momentary qualm. Johnson would never show emotion, no matter how thoroughly he was defeated.

"William, my boy!" Johnson cried ecstatically, pumping Hale's hand. His voice was as professionally hearty as ever. "And little Gloria—beautiful and charming as always! Ah, what joy it is to see you both after so long!"

"It's nice seeing you, too, *partner*!" said Hale. If Johnson observed Hale's emphasis, he didn't show it. He nodded and showed his false teeth in a grin of pleasure. "I must get a newspaper immediately," he said. "Come into the waiting room with me." And he began waddling away, almost at a run.

That, Hale thought, was the first slip. Jolly, as he seemed, Johnson couldn't entirely hide his concern. You bet he had to get a newspaper! To see where he could start wrecking, of course. Well, let him!

"Oh, before I forget," said Johnson, fumbling in the pockets of his tentlike overcoat. He handed two packages to Gloria and Hale.

"Congratulations, William, on your birthday, and on the magnificent job you've done. This is just a small token of my satisfaction—" Before Hale could answer, he had darted inside and was racing toward the newsstand.

"Isn't he *darling?*" gushed Gloria, fumbling with the string. "Why didn't you tell me it was your birthday, Billie-willie?"

"I...I forgot." The waiting room was comfortingly warm, but Hale was past noticing such trifles. Magnificent job? Certainly it was, but not from Johnson's point of view. What in hell did the devil mean?

Johnson held a paper wide open. "Ah, here it is," he said brightly. "Really, William, I had to hasten to get in at the kill. I left a number of interesting plans undeveloped, but I felt this was more important. Here—" He handed the paper to Hale, who read:

PAN-AMERICAN CREDIT CORP. IN TEM-PORARY RETRENCHMENT

The board of directors of the Pan-American Credit Corporation, in an official announcement, today gave out the information that momentary circumstances require a temporary restriction of

further credit for expansion of business.

This transitory situation, as an official spokesman for the corporation stated, should give rise to no misgivings. He warned that foreign interests, alarmed by the sudden gigantic productivity of the new world, might allege that in this briefly necessary action the Pan-American Credit Corporation, which is the largest coalition of its kind in the world, demonstrates lack of confidence in the future of the Americas.

Speaking in the most vigorous terms, the spokesman for the corporation stated emphatically that Pan-American has the utmost confidence in this hemisphere's capacity for unending expansion. The corporation's temporary action, he stated, is necessitated for a brief time by the increase of business inventories. He further stated that when these inventories are depleted somewhat, the corporation will embark on a credit policy even greater than in the past.

Hale returned the paper, smiling. How long would it take him to understand his enemy? What else could he expect from Johnson but a subtle attempt to demoralize him? But Lucifer, the supreme cheat, reduced to this pitiful wile! "What about it?" he demanded evenly.

"Splendid, William! One of my first tenets is never to appear other than a mere human being; always to seem to participate in the dominant human emotion of the moment."

"Come on, get to the point!"

Johnson looked uncertainly toward the highway entrance. "Have you brought the car?"

CHAPTER XXVIII

Hale nodded and started toward the door, but Gloria seized his arm. She had unwrapped her parcel. "Oh, look!" she squealed, holding up a golden looped cross. "What is it? It's *gorgeous!*"

Hale felt contempt for Johnson. Did Johnson think the object would scare him? A silly trick!

"The *ankh*," Johnson explained, guiding the Hales toward a door. "An excellent reproduction of one made for me by a superb Egyptian artisan...let me see...about four thousand years ago. The original was too valuable to keep. I acquired it very cheaply; the goldsmith was a fugitive— political trouble, you know, even in that time. A private collector paid me an exceedingly handsome price. Though yours were made by a modern Hindu craftsman, after a similar time you should also get a large price for yours—"

"But what *is* it?" Gloria insisted.

"The Egyptian symbol of eternal life."

"Oo!" Gloria quickly kissed Johnson's pudgy cheek. That was too much for Hale. Following them silently, he resolved that if Gloria wanted *him* to kiss her she'd have to scrub her mouth.

Johnson plopped into the soft seat, leaned forward, and closed the glass screen separating them from the chauffeur. The car started.

Hale said: "You don't have to pull that stuff on me. That article doesn't mean a thing! Sure, we have surpluses. People can't go on buying like maniacs all their lives. But as soon as Europe's settled, we'll have all we can do supplying them."

Johnson patted Hale's knee approvingly. "Excellent, William. However, I'm not a mortal who needs persuasion. We both know very well that at the moment munitions aren't

207

being accepted as a medium of exchange. And really, there is nothing else the former autocracies could offer. The dictators performed the most extraordinary feat. They plundered their nations of everything. Literally everything! You can't sell to people who have nothing to offer in exchange."

"We'll get out of it, all right," Hale said confidently. "We'll give credits to the rest of the world."

"You're testing me, aren't you, William?" Johnson's grin looked quite sincere, to Hale's irritation. "I'm afraid it isn't necessary. I understand your strategy quite well. But I won't spoil your fun."

He lit a cigar with his usual gestures. "I will admit that you've introduced into Hell a factor that I hadn't thought of. William, I must confess I am astonished at you. You seem to be a perfectly nice boy, and still you are capable of devising such utterly *diabolical* torments!

"I should never have been cunning enough—now, I mean; you can realize how one's mind grows dull with the passing millenia—to contrive it. Now, I must inform you, I haven't much longer to live. There is no need for both of us, since you have proved yourself a worthy successor."

Hale swallowed. Johnson went on, as if Hale had interrupted with a protest of modesty: "Yes, you probably don't consider yourself worthy. But you have tormented an entire hemisphere more efficiently than I have done in centuries; and soon the whole world will be involved, tortured more by their incomprehensible difficulties than even a war could have tormented them.

"Ah, William, you have done a beautiful job indeed! If I couldn't match it with a comparable accomplishment of my own—quite an old one, I confess; roughly five thousand years old—I should be inclined to envy you."

CHAPTER XXVIII

"Oh, cut it out!" snapped Hale. "I've defeated you, and you know it. Don't try to wiggle out of it."

"*I* try to wiggle out of it?" Johnson looked shocked. "Why, William, that's the last thing in the world I want to do. In a sense you *have* defeated me. Actually, though, you have shown yourself capable of succeeding me...as Lucifer!"

"What's the gag?" Hale fought to keep his temper.

"Now, boys," said Gloria, "don't quarrel!"

Johnson tapped the ash off his cigar with irritating composure. "Nothing of the sort, my dear.

"You see, William, *my* predecessor invented the instinct of self-preservation, thereby showing his ability. My own accomplishment was the discovery of hope. Both of these have increased the misery of Hell.

"But with your invention—*blind, senseless confidence*—there is almost no torment imaginable that can further augment man's suffering.

"He will continue producing to the limit of his endurance, regardless of the mounting surplus. He counts on extending credit to plundered nations, when you and I know that the Pan-American Credit Corporation hasn't a penny to lend them—"

"*What?* Don't be an ass! It has all the future to draw on. There's no limit to its credit!"

Johnson bobbed his white head admiringly. "Sinister, William, most sinister indeed! You showed far greater ingenuity than mine when you planted that insane confidence in their minds. They will believe in the limitless credit of the future, and never admit that the future has already been exhausted. There is no more credit, and we know why, eh,

William? Though we'll never convince your subjects."

"Yeah? Why?"

Johnson wagged a finger. "Don't pretend innocence! Everybody owes everybody else, and in turn is owed by everybody. Consequently it will be impossible to collect, which erases the possibility of credit. Incidentally, money will, I fear, be destroyed as a medium of exchange. That I regret, for I had an inordinate fondness for the pretty stuff; but as I shall go on to my reward soon, that is your concern.

"When money debts become uncollectable, money will have to be abandoned; and my opinion is that a highly industrialized, more impractical form of barter will complicate matters for the damned even further."

Hale sat quietly, chilled. "They can slow down production—"

"Ah, but they can't!" Johnson gazed at Hale with frank respect. "There you showed your astounding artfulness. They will never, never believe that their system of anarchic, geometrically increasing production is unworkable!

"Furthermore, you have adroitly removed all the natural checks on such insensate production. Formerly an employer could reduce his expenses and wait for his inventory to diminish. But now every man is his own employer. He can't very well throw himself out of work, can he?"

"He can stop producing for a while and just live on his savings."

"He has no savings. At any rate he won't when the system collapses under the weight of its surpluses, which should be some time this week. I'm glad I shall be here to see the crash; it will make the Battle of Troyes look like a backyard squabble."

Hale opened his mouth to protest some more. But what

could he say? Johnson's statements appeared to add up. And then he went on: "By proving yourself a worthy successor, William, you allow me to go on to my next existence. What it will be I don't know. But it can't help being more pleasant than this one, since this is Hell.

"Evidently we—those of us who are doomed, from time to time, to the supreme torment of indeterminate immortality as manager of Hell—committed the most unspeakable crimes in some other existence.

"While Hell would no doubt supply plenty of torment without our help, a manager is evidently required to assure the most efficient and economical distribution of misery.

"So this is our punishment. We must redeem ourselves with infinitely greater pain than any of the other damned souls.

"I have done so, at the cost of five thousand years of the most intense anguish: monotony, boredom, loneliness. You have escaped loneliness by your spell, but I greatly fear the cure will prove worse than the disease, if you will excuse the trite expression. I am unutterably tired and anxious for an end to my torment.

"However, I must warn you not to count on redemption within five millennia. Before you leave this place, you will be required to find and train a successor, one who deserves what eventually seems like eternal damnation.

"You will seize and discard any number before you strike one who is cursed as we are, for unspeakable crimes in those other planes are damnably rare, it seems.

"You will live in a perpetual agony of hope that each generation will deliver up your successor. And you will never know, until almost the last moment, when your successor is at hand, except by the most intensive search for him...or her! That could as easily be a million years—"

Hale's nerves had gone completely limp. There was no more rebellion in him. You get what you want, if you try hard enough—and then wish you hadn't. You can't escape first principles.

Victory was defeat. Why? Because: "By grasping the principle that *anything you do, irrespective of your intentions, will increase the misery and torments of the people,* you have confirmed my belief that you were to be my successor, for you understand that that is how Hell is constructed. If you didn't know it before, you do now, most emphatically!"

One hope had been smashed, the solitary hope that he might, by defeating Lucifer, escape relatively eternal torment. He had succeeded. What was the result of his victory? It bound him forever to his defeat. So far from defeating Lucifer, he had *become* Lucifer.

"I don't want—" he said. "I didn't intend—"

Johnson patted his arm sympathetically. "I know, my boy. That's the way it was with me, when I invented hope. That's the way it is with all of us. It's part of our fate." He sat back, puffing his cigar.

"Yes, William, I can never express my relief that I have not put my trust in you to no purpose. You were my last hope, and for a while I feared you were too nervous and temperamental for the job. If you had failed me, I don't know what I should have done.

"Ah, my boy, what gratification it gives me! Developing you, watching you, guiding you, to take my place as the supremely damned manager of Hell. In training you as my successor, I have not wasted thirty years!"

Hale was shocked erect. "Thirty years! You mean you

planned all this...Gloria and everything—"

"I'm sorry," Johnson reached across Hale's lap and took something from Gloria. "I see your eternal helpmate has unwrapped your birthday present." He put the second *ankh* in Hale's limp grasp. *"I mean thirty-two!"*

"Isn't it cute, Billie-willie?" cried Gloria.

Hale stared at the object. Billie-willie....Cute...The ankh, immortality, cute!

He sat, numbed and dumbly cold, staring at the bright, hard gold that symbolized his inescapable eternity of doom.

THE END